Legacy of Magick

By

Ellen Dugan

ACKNOWLEDGMENTS

Thanks to all my friends who have offered support, enthusiasm, and encouragement on this adventure. A special thank you goes to Tess and Katie for being my super, speed-reading, Beta readers, and to my editors Barbara and Meg. To Kyle for the fabulous cover art, thanks to Lenora and to Jeanne for talking me through the reality of revisions.

To CH and LH who had both once asked me, "Why in the world aren't you writing fiction?"

Finally, this book is dedicated with love to my husband Ken and our children, Kraig, Kyle and Erin. Who each reminded me to never let *anything* stand in the way of a dream.

CHAPTER 1

Now that's a house with charm. I'd just jogged back into my neighborhood, and over the tree line my aunt's house came into view. Jeez, it wasn't a house. It was a manor. Silver gray, trimmed in contrasting burgundy and white, and painted gingerbread. It had two towers shaped like pointed witch's hats.

It was views like this that made me love William's Ford, Missouri, my new home as of two weeks ago. The old, uneven, brick sidewalk beneath my feet, however, was another matter. I really had to mind my footing here— I snapped my head up. A man had stepped right in front of me.

"Hey!" I tried to step to the side to avoid him, but I was in mid-stride and we smacked solidly into each other. I shouted out a few choice words as I felt myself falling to the bricks.

I automatically put my hands out to stop my fall, and they fortunately hit the grass while one of my knees met the bricks. The only thing that kept me from fully face planting on the brick sidewalk was the man, who had wrapped his arms around me and angled us for the grass instead. We landed in a heap, and my breath rushed out in a solid thump. My sunglasses bounced and sat crookedly on my face. For a few seconds, we stayed down there with his arms wrapped around my waist.

With a groan, he rolled over and off to sit on the sidewalk next to me. I was still down on the ground, my right hip and knee had taken most of the impact. I glared at him. I started to move, and my initial fury at someone being stupid enough to get in my way, changed the moment I adjusted my glasses and got a clear look at him.

Oh, wow. If I had to be knocked flat by somebody, this was the one I would have chosen. He looked to be in his late twenties. He wore a coordinated jogging shirt and shorts in black and royal blue. His sandy blonde hair was short and a bit tousled. Bright blue eyes smiled at me as he started to apologize. Like me, he was wearing work out clothes and earbuds.

He pulled out his own earbuds to ask, "Are you all right? I'm sorry."

He looked me straight in the eyes. Well, okay, technically he looked straight into my sunglasses, but let me tell you, his *look* packed a punch. He climbed to his feet and stood up. Let's add tall to the list. He offered his hand in a friendly way, as I shifted off my hip to put one foot down flat so I could get to my feet.

I automatically took the offered hand, and he tugged

me the rest of the way up. I weirdly felt a jolt of energy when our palms connected. "Thanks." I said. Flustered, I did my best not to stare open-mouthed at this incredibly gorgeous guy... who still held onto my hand. He was toned with a summer tan. Wow. He apologized again.

"I am really sorry. I had my music up too loud and I didn't see you until the last minute. Are you sure you're okay?" He looked down at my knee. It was skinned up, but nothing major.

While I stood there trying to catch my breath, I felt little currents of energy rush up my arm from the hand he still held. As I belatedly pulled my hand away, the sensation stopped. *How weird is that?*

"Yeah, thanks to you throwing us mostly to the grass — instead of letting me fall on the sidewalk." I huffed out, as I brushed off my mismatched bright orange top and purple shorts. I was a little out of breath, both from the jogging and the collision. My own earbuds were dangling crazily, so I grabbed the ends and tried to act natural. As if running into gorgeous men, skinning my knee, and ending up tangled in their arms on the ground happened to me on a regular basis.

Who could blame a girl for being a little flustered?

"I'm Duncan Quinn." He introduced himself, and I felt my heart thump hard against my ribs.

"Autumn." I tried to introduce myself as smoothly as possible. But what could I do? Sweating, out of breath, and with no makeup on — I could only cringe as I imagined how I must look and smell. Crap. Was my deodorant working? Did I smell? Suddenly I realized that he was still talking to me and I almost missed what he was saying.

"—on the estate with my mother's family until I settle on a place of my own." he said.

"Oh," I replied lamely. Apparently falling to the ground had knocked the power of speech from my brain. I tried again.

Come on, Autumn, focus.

"So, you live around here?" I asked casually. Yes, I know I basically repeated what he said, but it was the best I could come up with. I reached up to pull my long brown hair into a tighter ponytail, and prayed that my hair was not sticking out all over the place.

He hooked a thumb over his shoulder and gestured to the large gothic-style stone manor house behind him. "Yeah, I live right there in the big stone mausoleum."

I peered up at the house, and it did seem a little creepy. It also seemed familiar, somehow. "Well, it was nice running into you," I said with an attempt at humor.

He laughed and I grinned at him. Hurray! My brain was working again. I was able to make clever conversation with an attractive man!

"So, do you live around here too?" He asked.

"A couple of blocks up the hill. It's not far."

"Why don't I walk you back to your house?" He asked me. "It's the least I can do." He glanced down at my knee with a frown.

"I think I'll live," I assured him.

"I'd feel better if I made sure you got home okay. It's not every day I knock a girl off her feet. Literally," he said straight-faced.

"You're a funny guy, Duncan." I chuckled, and started slowly walking back down the sidewalk as he fell into step by my side. At first, he seemed to be hovering, watching to see if I was alright, I supposed. For the next couple of blocks we walked easily together. I was sort of impressed when he commented about some of the other historic homes in the neighborhood. He knew his stuff, I realized, as he pointed out a federal style brick cottage and a few Queen Anne-style houses to me.

"You must be really into architecture,"

"Yeah," he admitted, "I studied architecture and historic preservation in college. It actually comes in handy in my line of work."

"What's your line of work?"

"I flip houses. Remodel and repair broken down homes, and I also restore older historical homes. My family is into real-estate," he pointed at a real estate sign in a yard across the street, with the agent's name listed as 'Rebecca Drake-Quinn'. "My mom backed me on my first flip a couple of years ago; I made a decent profit on the sale. I paid her back, and then bought my second house to flip on my own. And then I just kept on going."

Wait, the family name *Drake* rang a bell. He had said

that he lived on the family *estate*. After living here a couple of weeks, I thought about how many times I had seen the name 'Drake', both on local buildings and in the title of local businesses. There was even a hall named after the Drake family on the University campus. Which meant that, through his mother, he was part of the family that, apparently, had fingers in every business in town. A wealthy, connected family. I bet he'd be curious as to who *my* family was next. I wondered what his reaction would be when he found out I was a Bishop.

"I thought I knew most people in the neighborhood. Are you new here, a student maybe?" He asked, as I predicted.

I tried to sound casual and confident when I answered. "I recently moved here to stay with my father's family while I go to grad school."

He stopped walking and looked at me intently. "Who's your family?"

"The Bishops." I was braced for his reaction as my father's family was a little bit — *different.* So I watched him carefully.

"You're related to Gwen Bishop?" He seemed surprised as he studied my features.

"Yes, she's my aunt. Do you know her?" I asked.

His expression stayed neutral. "That means your father is Arthur Bishop."

"Yes, he passed away about a year and a half ago." I informed him.

"I'm sorry." He said gently.

"Thank you." I said.

We walked along quietly for a few moments. Well that was interesting. He seemed a little surprised, but other than that, very little reaction to the family.

I was relieved when he cheerfully picked the conversation back up.

"I know your cousin, Bran. I've been working with him. He's been helping me track down the original blueprints, at the university library, for some of the historic buildings I have been rehabbing." He said cautiously, as if he expected *me* to react.

I considered as we walked together. He had said buildings. As in more than one. This wasn't merely an average guy, or a general contractor. I peeked over at him as he pulled an expensive looking cell phone out of his pocket to check an incoming text. While he answered that, I discreetly checked him out again. That was name brand athletic apparel he was wearing and top-of-the-line jogging shoes too. The runner in me approved of the brand, even though I knew it was hideously expensive.

Rich guy. Definitely.

"Have you always lived here?" I asked.

"No. I went to an East coast prep school, and then Yale. After I got my degree, I ended up moving back to town permanently." He sounded resigned but grinned at me as we kept walking towards the manor.

I felt another little jolt of power and a connection as

I smiled back at him. So he was living with his family too. What a weird way to meet someone, but I was glad I decided to run this morning.

As we walked up to the front gates at the end of the manor's driveway, I pushed the black wrought iron gate open and turned to look up at him. His dark blonde hair was casually mussed, and his blue eyes were smiling. I almost sighed out loud. He seemed like a great guy, nice and friendly. I wondered how I could work out seeing him again.

Then it dawned on me that maybe he was simply being kind, and wasn't interested in me at all. He was probably being polite, with all that wealth, breeding, and so forth. It made me wonder if he had taken classes for these types of situations at that prep school? You know, "Damsel in Distress? Here's how to be a gentleman and still look hot!"

I bet he did. Crap. Oh well, grad school was going to take up most of my time starting next week anyway.

To my amazement he reached out and took my hand, not to shake it, just to hold. His other hand tipped my sunglasses playfully down. "You have green eyes." He smiled at that. "I wondered what I'd find behind those sunglasses."

"Yeah, I've had them forever." I managed not to stutter. "The eyes, I mean."

"Autumn, I really am glad I ran into you this morning."

Oh wow, I felt those little tingles again. And was this

guy smooth or what? I frantically tried to think of something clever to say; instead I stood there and stared at him. Like an idiot.

He pushed my glasses back into place with a fingertip, and let go of my hand. He bent down at the edge of the yard, and plucked a yellow daisy from the garden.

"Sorry. Again." He handed me the daisy.

"Thanks for walking me home," I finally managed.

"I'll see you around." He waved as he left. I stood there and watched him for a bit as he put his ear buds back in, and then as he jogged farther off, and down the street.

I grinned after him for a moment, and tucked the daisy behind my ear. I shut the gate, walked quickly up the driveway, and bounded up the front porch steps.

I let myself in the front door, closed it, and leaned back for a moment with a happy sigh. Suppressing a giggle, I headed to the kitchen for some water. I had a *feeling* I would be seeing him again and soon.

After all, he knew where I lived and I knew where he lived. Plus, I felt something between us; that jolt of energy and those tingles when we touched. That was new for me. I wondered what it meant, and I wondered if it would be lame to say I felt a sort of *connection* to him?

Attraction? Oh yeah. I had a hunch the attraction was more than one-sided (and I was good with hunches).

Hunches, dreams, and visions have been a part of my life for as long as I can remember. Even when I was small, I'd often known what the future would bring. I thought I had that pretty much under control most of the time. I am a Seer and I have what used to be called, back in the old days, "The Sight". Capital T. Capital S. And honestly, it is one ginormous pain in the ass.

I reached into the fridge to grab a bottle of water, and noticed that my knee and both of my palms were stinging. When I looked down, I saw a little rivulet of blood running down my leg. I grabbed a paper towel, and blotted my skinned knee, just as I heard footsteps on the kitchen stairs.

Knowing the rest of the family would be up soon, I figured I had a decent shot at getting to the hall bathroom for a shower before my seventeen year old, twin cousins woke up and took it over. I had learned after a few days that my oldest cousin, Bran, had his own bathroom, which he did *not* share. Aunt Gwen had the largest bedroom on the second floor that boasted a curved sitting area and a huge, private en-suite bathroom.

But I didn't mind sharing with the twins. They seemed to be pretty likable teenagers, even though the bathroom was usually an explosion of towels, toiletries, and makeup. It sort of reminded me of when I had lived in the dorms, back when I was an undergrad.

I saw with some surprise, Holly, the oldest of the twins, come bouncing down the steps.

Holly's curly reddish-blonde hair was pulled back in a neat ponytail to leave her heart-shaped face unframed. Large, aqua-blue eyes blinked as she noticed me standing at the counter, sweating and chugging water.

Holly stood at the bottom of the steps, wearing her orange one piece swimsuit, athletic shorts, and flip flops, while holding a duffle bag. She looked cool, calm, and pretty as usual. However, Holly reeked of sunscreen, which was easy to explain. Holly had been working at the country club pool this summer as a lifeguard, while Ivy pitched in at the family's bookstore. Then I remembered that today was Holly's last official day of work at the pool. She had to be up early as well.

Holly's eyes zeroed in on the paper towel in my hand and the blood stain. She dropped her bag and knelt down in front of my knee.

"Autumn, what did you do?" She asked.

"It's only a skinned knee." I rolled my eyes at her. "I've had worse."

"Let me see it." Holly wrapped her hand around my leg firmly. For all the sympathy, her grip was strong. Resigned to her inspection, I shut my mouth and stood there. There was no point in arguing with her, she could be amazingly stubborn.

As I watched, Holly closed her eyes and *looked*. She went very still as her attention focused internally on whatever her senses told her. She cocked her head to one side, as if she was listening or concentrating. Her hand trailed up to my hip and hovered over the area where I had fallen. Then her aqua-blue eyes opened again and aimed directly up at me.

"It doesn't hurt too much right now, but you're going to be sore tomorrow. Also your stomach feels all jittery and fluttery," she looked at me and waited.

With a sigh I gave in, "Someone accidentally ran into me while I was jogging. I'm fine."

"He knocked you down. You took the impact on your palms, your right hip, and your knee." Holly stated firmly. She didn't guess, she *knew*.

I tipped my sunglasses down to squint at her. "Witch." I accused her teasingly.

"Yes, I am." She grinned cheerfully up at me.

As I'd only recently learned, all of the weird experiences I'd dealt with my whole life— the dreams that came true, my very accurate hunches, even seeing the future— was part of my family legacy. Some people inherited blue or brown eyes, but in my father's family, the children all inherited paranormal powers. I got The Sight (hence the whole 'Seer' thing). Or, if you want to get technical, I was a clairvoyant.

Apparently, my father had been a Witch, but I'd never known while he was alive. It had been a bit of a jolt to discover that I came from a witchcraft prone family.

"Is he cute?" Holly wanted to know.

I raised an eyebrow at her question. "You tell me if he's cute or not."

Holly stood and looked at me carefully. "I am an empath, Autumn. Not a clairvoyant. I can sense your injuries and physical pain and feel your emotions, but I can't see a picture of him in my head." She said patiently.

"I'll tell you all about it later," I promised. "Right now, I really want to hit the shower before Ivy gets up and hogs the hall bathroom."

"He must be cute, because you have some pretty excited and happy feelings for the guy who knocked you down." Holly grinned at me as she fished her own sunglasses and car keys out of her bag.

"Mind your own business," I suggested. "Go be a lifeguard or something." I gestured with the water bottle, and lifted it to my mouth for a swig.

Holly calmly walked to the back door with a little smirk. "Don't forget to put that flower he gave you in some water. I have a feeling you'll want to keep it."

I choked on the water I'd been guzzling and glared as my cousin headed off to work. I heard her giggling at getting in the last word. Once I stopped coughing, I chucked the empty water bottle in the recycle bin, and realized that trying to keep anything a secret in this house was going to be basically impossible.

Well, they were all Witches. I laughed to myself. *What can you do?*

CHAPTER 2

I did manage to take that shower before Ivy even got out of bed. Feeling smug at getting the bathroom first, I wrapped myself in a big towel, and started out the door to find my cousin waiting and leaning against the wall opposite the bathroom doorway. Her eyes were half closed, and basically she looked annoyed at the world in general.

She wore a black tank with skull and crossbones patterned pajama shorts. Her tangled, dyed black hair was sort of sticking up straight in the air. There were circles of smeared black eye makeup under both her green eyes, which made her look like a gothic raccoon. Somebody had slept in their makeup again.

"'Morning, sunshine." I smirked as I strolled past her.

"Don't mess with me," She warned. "Need caffeine to function at this ungodly hour of the day." She staggered into the bathroom, and the untouched door slammed behind her.

Ivy did everything with dramatic flair, I was going to have to get used to that.

A half hour later, my contacts were in, my makeup was on, and my long hair was brushed back into a low pony tail that hung straight down my back. When it was this hot outside, leaving my hair loose simply drove me crazy. My palms stung slightly and my hip and knee were a bit sore, but otherwise I was feeling okay.

I was seated at the old oak kitchen table wearing black and white Ikat print shorts, a black scoop neck t-shirt, and my aqua colored gladiator sandals. I had sliced up a banana into my cereal and was having breakfast with my Aunt Gwen. My older cousin, Bran, was seated at the table as well, reading the newspaper and looking buttoned up and proper as usual.

And he was ignoring me. Again. As usual.

Merlin, the family's cat, was sitting in the empty kitchen chair beside me. His white paws were on the edge of the table and he seemed to be keeping an eye on the kitchen. Either that or he was reading Bran's newspaper. Honestly, I wouldn't put it past him.

Merlin was a solid fifteen pounds of long, lean, and muscular cat. Except for a little star shaped patch of white on his chest and the tips of his front paws, he was solid black. The first time I saw the white star in his black fur I thought it was a trick. That cat is so strong he has dog toys to play with. Seriously. Merlin *adopted* me two weeks ago as soon as I had unpacked my first box here at my aunt's house. He hopped out of my aunt's arms, started exploring all of the boxes I brought, and had been my shadow ever since.

Seeing this little domestic scene, you'd never guess at the extraordinary abilities of the family. The Bishops held successful jobs and were active in their local schools and business community. They had regular friends, maintained a gorgeous house, and tended amazing gardens. Once you got past the jolt of "We're Witches," my father's family was, for lack of a better word, relatively *normal.*

Aunt Gwen was speaking to the both of us about the store and what she wanted to get accomplished today. First on the list: inventory.

"You and Ivy should be able to go through the book stock, the herbs, and the crystals easily enough." She paused as she sipped some herbal tea. Gwen wore a flowing purple dress and, as she lowered her teacup, silver rings sparkled on every finger. "That is, if she decides to join us today." She smirked a few seconds later when Ivy shuffled into the kitchen.

Ivy's face was now clean of makeup. She was wearing a dark red bath robe, and a crimson headband was tucked over her freshly washed hair. With her pale complexion, black hair, and the blood red robe, I thought that she looked like a vampire who had gotten up out of the wrong side of the coffin.

Beside me, Aunt Gwen choked a little on her tea.

Crap. Was Aunt Gwen was telepathic? Wouldn't that suck if she could read my mind? You know, literally hear my thoughts! Aunt Gwen glanced over at me with laughter in her eyes, as if to confirm my suspicions.

Note to self: add telepathy to the list of Aunt Gwen's witchy talents.

Second note to self: Read up on psychic abilities, ASAP.

I smiled back at my aunt who was trying not to chuckle, and sat back in my chair to watch the show. No one speaks to Ivy in the morning, unless they have a death wish. She's really not a morning person, so the vampire analogy was pretty apt.

We watched as Ivy went straight to the refrigerator and grabbed a can of diet soda. She opened the can and chugged the soda with one hand on her hip, while she stood in front of the fridge with the door wide open.

"You are refrigerating the entire house, dear." Aunt Gwen said calmly.

Ivy's head was tipped back, and she was guzzling that caffeine laden soda as if her life depended on it. While she was still chugging, she stepped back a few paces and the untouched refrigerator door closed smartly all on its own. Which I admit, made me flinch.

"Show-off," Bran accused her, turning a page in the paper. Merlin gave a huge feline yawn, and Aunt Gwen merely chuckled.

Ivy's talent was telekinesis. She could make inanimate objects move. Typically, it was little things. Pictures rattling on the wall, dishes in the cupboards, so most people never noticed. As she had gotten older, she had learned some control, she told me. But if she was tired, aggravated, or scared, items would move more violently. As in the more wound up she was, the more force would be generated. This morning Ivy's mood apparently was... pissy.

Ivy finally stopped the soda chugging and came up for air. I tried not to laugh as she stalked over to the table, pulled out a chair with a frown, and sat. Ivy deliberately placed the soda can off to the side, and then folded her arms on the table. She sighed and let her head fall down to her crossed arms with a dramatic *thud*.

"Really, Ivy," My aunt shook her head and added a *tsk- tsk.* "We should sign you up for acting classes."

"It's early," Ivy whined. This was somewhat muffled, as she was basically talking to the table top.

"Aren't we the drama queen this morning?" I said as I went to put my now empty cereal bowl in the dishwasher.

Ivy rolled her head to the side and glared at me. The spoon I had left on the table started to quiver. Unaffected by this, Aunt Gwen scooped it up and handed it to me to add to the other dishes.

Trying to take stock of the goings on around me, I tried not to let my surprise show as I studied the fragrant herbs drying from a brass curtain rod above the kitchen sink.

Normal? Had I granted the family *relatively normal*?

I shook my head at myself while I loaded up the

dishwasher, the familiar scent of drying rosemary and thyme perfuming the air was homey and calming. I supposed Ivy's more theatrical magickal talents might frighten some people, but the effect this morning was somewhat dampened by the fact that she currently had her head down on the kitchen table, like a little kid.

"Mom, can't I go in at noon instead of nine o'clock this morning?" She whined.

Aunt Gwen patted her on the head as she rose. "We are leaving for the store in twenty minutes, Ivy. You can be ready and ride with us or you can walk," she announced quietly, but firmly.

"Fine," Ivy grumbled. She sat up, yawned hugely, and grabbed her soda again. "I'll go put a face on."

"Twenty minutes, Ivy." Aunt Gwen warned her as she looked through the cream colored kitchen cabinets on the far side of the kitchen.

Ivy muttered under her breath, but jogged quickly back up the stairs. Bran stood up. With his neatly cut red hair, and deep green eyes, he was very GQ handsome in a bookish kind of way. Well, until he opened his mouth and you discovered how pompous he was. His lips curved up a bit as he announced, "Mom, remember I have a faculty meeting later today, then Angela and I are going to the theater. So I won't be home this evening."

I inwardly sneered at the thought of his girlfriend. I'd only met Angela once, and she seemed very much the upper crust society type, plus she'd been just as patronizing as Bran. So they were perfect for each other, in my opinion.

As I turned the dishwasher on, I was startled to see my cousin smile. When he did I had a sudden flash of him, looking all dapper, and handsome in a tuxedo. *He stood there beaming by an evergreen tree that was lit up with white sparkling lights, and covered in gold star shaped ornaments.* Then the perspective on the vision shifted, *and a woman wearing a long white dress walked down the manor stairs towards him.* Her face was hidden by a veil, so I couldn't see her, but the expression on his face was enough for me to know. Bran was going to be married. By the end of the year, judging by the Christmas tree in the vision.

The vision faded away and I found myself standing in the kitchen staring at my cousin. I shivered a bit and pressed a hand to my suddenly queasy stomach as I came back to the present time. I felt a little rush sweep over me from the force of what I had just *seen.*

The vision had only lasted a couple of seconds, but wow, it had been intense! Apparently The Sight had decided to come out and play today. I blinked my eyes and shook my head a bit to clear out the images. I went straight to the nearest kitchen chair and sat down, very deliberately.

"What?" He frowned at me.

No way was I telling him about what I had seen. Instead I said, "That's the first time I have seen you smile since I moved here. Must be the thought of getting some action tonight that has you all chipper."

He rolled his eyes at me and walked out of the kitchen, muttering to himself about being plagued by another smart ass in the family.

"So, Autumn," My aunt turned back to me holding what looked to be a first aid kit and an unlabeled bottle holding some kind of liquid. If she had noticed anything, or suspected that I'd just had a vision, then she covered it very well, which made me figure, that she hadn't. "Tell me about the young man you met this morning." She sat next to me and put my foot in her lap to better doctor my, now slightly gooey, knee.

"Did you overhear Holly and me talking?" I asked as I held the open kit, and she rooted through it.

"No, but I did have a dream about you meeting someone new," she said as she tucked her lightly silver-streaked, auburn hair neatly behind her ear. I saw that she had on crescent moon earrings today. "I also foresaw a silly accident," she looked at me with one eyebrow raised. "I assume he is the reason you have a scraped knee?"

Aunt Gwen looked a bit peeved, but was still speaking pleasantly. She dabbed my knee with something, I assumed was homemade, out of the glass bottle. I expected it to sting, but it didn't. Next she got out a big bandage and quickly covered the area. So while she competently worked on my knee, I filled her in and assured her that it was simply an accident, and that no, he didn't hurt me at all. He actually was sweet and had walked me home.

"Duncan Quinn?" She asked me after I finished telling her about my morning adventure.

"Yes, he seemed really nice." I said, and took my foot out of her lap.

"Well, well..." Aunt Gwen hummed thoughtfully. "Rebecca Drake's son makes his move."

"Wait." I put a hand on her arm to stop her as she turned away. "Do you know Duncan?"

"I knew his mother." Aunt Gwen said cautiously after a moment. She stood up, walked over to the cabinet, and put the bottle and the first aid box away.

"He said his family was into real estate but that he restored and flipped houses." I told her. And that got me no response. "He didn't seem thrilled about living in that big old stone house, he called it a mausoleum," I added. Aunt Gwen still didn't answer me. She seemed lost in her own thoughts.

I fiddled with the bandage on my knee and waited for her to reply. As I waited for my aunt's response, I started to feel a tightening in my stomach. I got the sinking feeling that there was something here that she that didn't want me to know. While I ruminated over that, Merlin hopped up into my lap to knead and purr.

Aunt Gwen knelt down and placed her right hand on my skinned knee. She took a controlled breath and I felt her fingers grow warm while they sat lightly on top of the bandage. I waited while she repeated a quiet healing charm over it. After she finished, she patted me on the leg. "We'll talk about it later."

"So, that healing thing you just did? That was pretty cool." I rubbed a hand over Merlin's kitty head for courage, and then I asked her what I'd been working up to for days. "Will you teach me about the family's legacy? You know, the magick part."

I watched my aunt's face light up. "We'll begin with magickal theory and the basics of the Craft, right away."

"When will you teach me how to do spells?" I wanted to know.

She raised an eyebrow at me. "After you have a bit of time and study under your belt, perhaps later this year."

I sighed in disappointment.

"I think you'll find helping out at the shop educational. You can learn a lot about the tools and supplies of the Craft there." Aunt Gwen gathered up her purse and paperwork for the day.

For some reason, I frowned after my aunt. I had to wonder... was she stalling? Why wouldn't she teach me any spells?

Now, I did not consider myself very empathic. I couldn't feel emotions like my cousin Holly could, but, Witch or not, everybody has instincts. And mine were screaming that something was definitely up. Which made me wonder, since I had just experienced a waking vision about Bran, if maybe mine were ratcheted up a few notches? There was a noticeable tension in my aunt that wasn't there a few moments ago. I also had the distinct feeling that Aunt Gwen was concerned, and that she did not approve of Duncan Quinn. But why?

My musings were cut short as Bran walked back in the kitchen to retrieve his briefcase. Ivy trailed behind him, grumbling. So I got up, which annoyed the cat, then snagged my own purse, and followed them out through the conservatory, filled with green plants and herbs, and finally out to the garage.

"I'd like to talk to you later, anyway." I said to my aunt as I walked past Bran and stood by the passenger door of Gwen's car. "I've been having some creepy dreams for weeks, and I'd like you to help me figure them out."

"About what?" Ivy asked around a huge yawn.

"Running through a cemetery. I'm with someone, but I can't see their face. It's night and I'm afraid, and there's an overwhelming sense of urgency to the dream..." I shuddered. *God I hated cemeteries.*

"You can't interpret the basics on your own, cousin?" Bran asked as he hit the button on the garage door opener. He was smiling when he said that, but anyone would have felt the condescension that was coming off of him in waves. "I could interpret dreams by the time I was ten." He slid into his practical sedan and started the engine. I had to resist the urge to flip him the bird.

As Ivy climbed in the back seat, Gwen smiled reassuringly at me over the hood of her car. "Of course, honey. We can do that right after dinner tonight."

"Thanks," I said. I chose to ignore Bran and his typical superior attitude. No way was I going to tell Bran about my *seeing* him getting married. Good grief, he'd be even more impossible to live with.

If such a thing were even possible.

***

I helped Ivy with the inventory and we accomplished quite a bit. Aunt Gwen stayed closed in her office with catalogues, getting ready to order items for the fall season and the holidays. Whenever Ivy and I had a moment alone, I tried to get more information about Duncan Quinn and why Aunt Gwen seemed to be unhappy about him and me meeting each other. Ivy didn't have much to say on the topic and the shop was busy that morning.

In between my other tasks, I people watched, which in a metaphysical store was a pretty entertaining past time. I felt a little out of my depth in the shop, and I referred the customers to Ivy for any questions. In most stores, employees couldn't wear a black t-shirt that proclaimed 'Come to the Dark Side. We have cookies!' along with a red and black lace choker, long red plaid shorts and heavy black boots. But at Enchantments, it worked.

I did learn by listening and watching Ivy's adept handling of the clientele. By paying attention to the customers and their purchases, I learned that black tourmaline was the stone of choice for protection, while rose quartz was preferred for romance. As I counted out the little mini spell candles, I noted the framed list of each color's magickal uses that was alongside the display. Well that was interesting. I had always loved candles, but my mother had forbidden them in the house. When I finished counting them all, I discreetly took out my cell phone, and snapped a picture of what the colors were each used for.

"Excuse me, darlin', can you help me?" said a southern voice behind me.

I tucked my phone in my back pocket, mildly embarrassed to have been caught taking a picture of the chart. I turned to discover a pretty, curvy woman with long dark hair, who was covered in the most amazing tattoos. Down both arms, across the back of her hands, and over her upper chest, they went in a stunning mishmash of colors and patterns. I said to her, "I'm new here, but I'll try."

"You Autumn? Gwen's niece that moved here from out east?" She inquired.

"Yes—" I began.

"Hey, I'm Marie." She took a deep breath and proceeded to tell me that she was opening up a tattoo shop right across the street.

I had to grin. Marie talked even faster than I did. Ivy practically materialized at my elbow, clearly she and Marie knew each other well, and the two of them began an animated discussion on the new shop. After swapping stacks of business cards, apparently they were going to cross promote, Marie inquired about Hoodoo herbs. She handed Ivy a list, and curious, I followed along to see what sort of herbs qualified as Hoodoo.

"High John root, vandal root, black snake root... yeah we have all of these." Ivy read the list off and went to the big glass apothecary style jars on shelves behind the counter and started pulling labeled jars down. Then she stopped. "Sorry, we don't have yellow dock in stock."

"Yellow dock?" I asked. "That's a wildflower. I saw some blooming along the jogging trail this week."

Marie tilted her head and looked at me. "How'd you know that?"

"My father ran a nursery and a landscape business. I used to work with him. I know plants." I explained to Marie and Ivy nodded at me in approval.

"You got time to show me where those plants are?" Marie asked.

"Well actually, the spot isn't far from here at all. It's really close. We could walk there, and be back shortly." I told Marie, as Ivy bagged and then rang up the herbs.

Marie tucked her wallet back into a huge bag, snagged her purchases and then hooked me by the arm. "You're on break. " She announced to Ivy. "I'll bring her back in a few." Then to me, Marie winked and said, "Let's go."

Ivy laughed and shooed us out the door. I guessed I

was going for a quick walk with Marie.

"So how do you like our town?" Marie asked, as we walked around the corner and headed towards the park, behind the shop.

"It's a little different from what I'm used to," was the best answer I could give her.

Marie grinned at me. "I bet so." She patted my arm. "Seemed to me, you needed a break from your aunt's shop. You feeling a bit overwhelmed. Too much to learn, eh?"

I didn't even bother to ask her how she knew.

A few moments later. we stood on the walking trail and I pointed out the six foot tall blooming stalks of yellow dock. "It's also called prairie dock in this part of the country. It likes to grow in dry waste areas." I explained.

The yellow dock was growing opposite of the wooded side of the trail, next to a parking lot. It was surrounded by weeds, and was in a spot where no one would mind if it was harvested. Marie produced a large pocket knife from the depths of her purse, and she neatly snipped a few leaves from the base and a dozen flowers from the tall stems.

I had almost offered to gather the plant material for her, but she clearly knew what she was about, as she only took a small amount of the plant. Business concluded we headed back towards Main Street.

"So, Marie, tell me about Hoodoo herbs..." I began.

"Girl, you and me? We are gonna be friends. " Marie

let loose a booming laugh.

I enjoyed listening as Marie gave me a run down on Hoodoo, she also called it root working, as we walked back Main Street. She handed me her business card and surprised me with a parting hug. I watched Marie hustle back across the street into a storefront where the sign said 'Opening Soon!'

It seemed that I was surrounded by magick. It was comforting and funny all at the same time. "Interesting characters you guys have in this town." I said to Ivy, as I let myself back into Enchantments.

"You don't know the half of it." Ivy warned me.

I went back over and resumed my counting of the various candles. "I swear, a Druid could walk in here, in full ceremonial garb, and I wouldn't even blink." I muttered to myself.

"Ha!" Ivy said from across the shop. "They dress like everyone else. Most the time."

I shook my head. Somehow, I knew she was going to say that.

CHAPTER 3

Aunt Gwen was so pleased with the progress that we had all made, and happy with finishing her fall ordering, that she ordered pizza for lunch for Ivy and me. Gwen announced that she and her friend Cora O'Connell, whose flower shop sat next door, were going out and that she was leaving Ivy and me in charge.

"If you need anything, call my cell. We'll be at the deli down the street." Aunt Gwen laid some money on the counter for the pizza delivery guy, and cheerfully walked out.

Ivy and I broke down a few packing boxes and emptied the garbage, while we waited for lunch to arrive. I volunteered to take out the trash and put it in the dumpster behind the shop. As I opened the back door, I heard a top volume argument coming from behind the shop next door.

Violet O'Connell stood on the back steps of the building next door, surrounded by fallen boxes of

flowers, and cursed her younger brothers in rapid fire...
something. Was that Gaelic? Both of the adolescents
stood there, with their heads down, and held their
skateboards. I supposed they had gotten busted for
skateboarding in the back parking lot.

My lips twitched. I had no idea exactly what she
was saying but the tone was universal. Violet had really
let loose on them. I wondered why.

I had met Violet briefly the first time I came to the
shop. I liked her. She was a couple of years older than
me, and she had recently become partners with her
mother in the family business. Outside of work, she, her
mother, and my aunt were also all in a coven together.

Violet seemed like she was fun and feisty, but boy,
did she have a temper. It sounded like her brothers were
getting a taste of it, right now.

I waved at them as I hauled the trash bag to the
dumpster.

"Autumn!" Violet waved me over. "Can you come
give me a hand?"

I tossed the bag toward the open dumpster, went
over, and reached for the nearest cardboard box. The
smell of roses overpowered me and a picture popped in
my head of a wedding gown. Ah ha! I had a hunch why
Violet was so frantic.

"Wedding flower shipment?" I asked her as we
scooped up the fallen boxes.

"Yes. It must have been a new delivery man. They
never leave the flowers on the back steps." Violet

pulled up the lid on the boxes and groaned to discover many of the flower heads of the white roses had snapped off from the long stems.

"Kevin and I didn't know they were back there," her brother, Eddie, said in their defense.

"All we did was open the door. The boxes all went crashing down the steps on their own!" Kevin piped up.

"Oh no." I quickly pulled up the lids on the other boxes as Violet stared at the damage.

"These boxes don't seem so bad," I said. I only counted a couple of snapped roses in the other boxes. The other flowers were all in shades of yellow and orange. But the white roses had taken the worst of it.

"They were out here in the heat for too long." Violet told me. "They are starting to open too much. I have to get them processed and cooled off— fast— to keep the blooms tight."

I reached for my cell phone in the pocket of my shorts. "Do you want me to call Gwen and have her tell your mom about the flower shipment?"

"No! Mum rarely gets to leave the shop. She was so happy to go out to lunch with Gwen today. If too many flowers are ruined we could have a big problem on our hands. This weekend's bride is a real Bridezilla." Violet dragged her hands through her hair.

Okay, maybe I could help. "Kevin, Eddie, go run next door. Tell Ivy what's happening and that I'm going to help Violet for a while."

The boys took off like a shot, ready to get away from

their older sister's wrath. I picked up two of the boxes and braced the back door open so Violet could bring all of the other boxes in.

My cell phone rang while we wrestled flower boxes inside. That would be Ivy. "Yeah?" I asked as I balanced the boxes I held, with the phone tucked under my ear.

"So... what do you want me to do with the rodents?" She asked about Violet's brothers.

"Can you keep them out of trouble for a while?" I asked as we hauled the boxes to the back design table in the shop.

"Yeah, the pizza's here. I could feed them," she suggested.

"Good. Send a few slices over here and I'll see if I can help Violet save the wedding flower shipment."

"You got it," Ivy said. Then I heard, "Don't even think about riding that skateboard in here!" Ivy continued to threaten the boys as she hung up.

Violet handed me a green apron, "Here put that on or you will ruin your shirt. This will be a messy job." She warned, as she blew her bangs out of her eyes. I saw that she had her eyebrow pierced and there were streaks the same color as her name in her blonde hair. A colorful sleeve of tattoos started at her right elbow and disappeared under her shirt sleeve.

I did as directed, and we spent the next half hour quickly cutting stems, stripping foliage and putting the flowers into the tall buckets filled with water and floral food solution. I actually loved helping Violet as we quickly worked on the flowers. She had an irreverent humor and regaled me with horror stories about their current Bridezilla.

At Violet's direction I hauled the flower filled tall buckets into the walk-in cooler and arranged them neatly side by side. She was right about wearing the apron. Who knew the fancy flowers you got from the florist were so messy? I had worked landscaping with my father for years. I knew dirty jobs. I also helped design, plant and maintain the flower beds at the landscape center and at my parent's house and we sure got grubby.

But these were fancy, expensive flowers for somebody's wedding. For some reason I thought working with flowers would be — I don't know — tidy, neat, clean, or something. However, they did smell terrific. There was something enchanting about the scent, color, and energy of them. Plus, the wedding flowers seemed to have a magick and a hopeful vibe all of their very own.

Fortunately for us it had stayed fairly quiet in the shop. We chatted while we cleaned up and finally ate. She told me about becoming a partner with her mother and I told her about my upcoming classes. No customers came in and the phone stayed silent while we worked to 'process' the wedding flowers, as Violet told me it was called.

We had finished and were stacking the empty boxes

as her mother, Cora, and Aunt Gwen strolled through the door.

My aunt did a double take, when she saw me wearing the flower shop's apron. "Autumn, what happened?"

"There was a little problem with the flower shipment..." I started to say and Violet rushed in to explain to her mother what had transpired while she was out to lunch.

"Why didn't you call me?" Cora demanded.

"I'm supposed to be your partner now, and I wanted you to have some time off and to enjoy yourself." Violet said.

"Where are your brothers?" Her mother demanded, sounding suspicious.

"Autumn sent them over to stay with Ivy."

At Violet's answer, my aunt closed her eyes and muttered something about the four horsemen of the apocalypse. Gwen moved quickly and went directly next door to check on her own shop. I hoped it was still standing. But with Ivy in charge, riding herd on two middle school boys, who knew? She'd probably started skateboarding with them. Inside the shop.

"Let's see what we have here." Cora strode forward and poked her head in the cooler.

I stood by Violet, and resisted the urge to wring my hands.

Mrs. O'Connell came out of the cooler a moment later. "You did a good job. It was smart to move quickly to minimize the damage."

"What about all those broken roses?" I asked Mrs. O'Connell.

"I can easily use those for boutonnières and corsages. There are enough long stems left for the bride's bouquet." She waved my concern away and headed for her office in the back of the shop. "But for now I need to make a phone call to my supplier and have a little talk about the new delivery man."

I bet that delivery man's ears would be blistered by time Mrs. O'Connell got through with him. A few moments later we could hear her mother having a *little talk* and we both started to grin. When the store's main phone rang, Violet went to grab it. I finished straightening the counters up, as Violet took an order for a delivery.

The bells over the flower shops door chimed, and as the door opened I turned to look automatically. To my amazement, Duncan Quinn and another man walked in the store. Duncan and I stood there and stared at each other for a few seconds. I felt a little tingle again.

"We have to stop meeting like this," he said seriously. He was dressed in old jeans, heavy work boots, and a snug dark blue t-shirt. He must have come from a job site.

"People are going to start talking," I joked.

"Do you work here?"

"No. I was helping out a friend with flowers that came in for a wedding today."

Then, I saw his companion look me over from head to toe. I tried not to flinch, but there was something *dismissive* about the way the other guy looked at me, like I was beneath him or something. I saw his gaze travel down to my legs. *Was this guy checking me out?*

"Nice sandals," he smirked at the aqua gladiator sandals on my feet.

"I like bright colors," I defended my choice automatically.

"Can I help you?" Violet asked them so politely that it sounded nasty. I glanced at her in surprise, as she hung up the phone. Then I watched as she swung her gaze to Duncan, and then to the other guy with an openly hostile expression.

"Violet," I introduced the two of them, "This is Duncan Quinn. He and I… ran into each other this morning." I looked at Duncan to introduce me to his friend.

"This is my cousin, Julian Drake."

Julian stared at me in an I'm-better-than-you-are sort of way that reminded me all too much of my cousin Bran. He, in contrast to his cousin, was wearing a suit and tie, that was cut in a way that let you know it was custom made and expensive. He had darker hair than Duncan, was a bit shorter, and more muscular. Julian was built like a weight lifter, while Duncan was thinner, taller, and basically built like a runner.

While I could see some family resemblance in their features, any similarity ended there. While Duncan was friendly, Julian radiated arrogance. Clearly he thought he was better than everybody else. As I watched him sneer at a few floral displays in the shop, for a second I thought I saw deep red field of energy floating around him, like I was looking at his aura.

When I realized what I was seeing, I jumped a little. I did not usually see auras around people unless I really worked at it. It was something else I'd tried to keep under control over the years. I blinked and then the color was gone.

Duncan nodded politely at Violet. "Hi Violet. My mother's birthday is today. I wanted to get her some flowers."

"Certainly." Violet said with a smile that showed all teeth and no warmth.

Feeling out of the loop, I decided to retreat. "I better get back to the shop and help out Ivy and Aunt Gwen. Let me get out of the way." I said to Violet, as I took off the apron. I snuck a peek at Duncan's cousin again. He looked normal except for the constant sneer. Had I imagined seeing his aura?

"Thanks for helping." She turned her back on the men to take the apron, and raised her eyebrows at me. The questioning look on her face said it all.

"I'll tell you later," I whispered. Then I nodded politely to Duncan and his cousin. "Bye." I said, as I attempted a casual and sophisticated exit out the front door of the shop. In other words, without tripping on anything.

"Blessed be," Violet called after me.

I clearly heard Julian snicker after me as I left.

Jerk! I walked down the sidewalk and opened the door of Enchantments, fully expecting pandemonium, only to discover Kevin and Eddie O'Connell quietly sitting on the floor, each with clipboards, happily counting out the number of tumbled stones in bins.

Ivy was ringing up a customer, while Aunt Gwen measured out dried herbs for another person. Peace and serenity ruled the store as Celtic music played softly in the background. I had to wonder if Ivy had cast a spell on those two rowdy boys.

I walked behind the counter as the customer took her shopping bag and moved to the door. "Have any trouble with Kevin and Eddie?" I said quietly to Ivy.

"Nope. After they ate pizza, they started doing the inventory on the tumbled stones and crystals." Ivy replied in a mater of fact tone.

"Jeez! What did you do, mind control on them or something?" I joked.

Ivy whipped her head up. "You wouldn't know, but it is not ethical to work magick that impedes another person's free will. It's also against the rules to work magick on another person without their permission."

"Oh." I said. Wasn't that interesting? I hadn't known that.

"Besides, I didn't have to resort to magick." Ivy wiggled her eyebrows at me and grinned. "I bribed them."

I had to laugh. "With what?"

"I promised to go to the skate park with them later and watch them practice." She confided back in a whisper, so only I could hear.

Aunt Gwen moved to the register to ring up her customer. "Be sure to wear your helmet, when you skateboard this afternoon, dear," she said calmly.

I jumped, and Ivy only shrugged. You'd think I would start to get used to it by now. But Aunt Gwen still caught me off guard. I was also starting to recognize that I really needed to learn more about telepathy: pronto.

"I'll go see if I can help them finish up." Ivy headed over to help the boys.

I took a clipboard myself and went to the rack of greeting cards to start counting. I wondered about Duncan and his jerk of a cousin, Julian. I was a little surprised at myself and my instant reaction. But there was something about that other guy that I truly did not like.

I told myself to focus, and looked down at the list. Aunt Gwen had the card inventory separated by the company, the design, and the price of each card. All I had to do was count them, which was going to be hard to do given the disarray of the greeting cards. So, I set the clipboard down and started pulling the cards out of the rack. These cards were so pretty, with lots of magickal and mystical artwork and designs. But they were totally mixed up.

As I organized them, I looked up to see Violet's brothers leaving and waved at them as they headed out. I was getting ready to start counting cards when I saw Duncan Quinn. He was standing outside of the door, frowning through the glass, and into our shop.

A moment later he opened the door and let himself in. I was fairly hidden behind the card racks so I had the chance to watch him and his expression as he came inside. I was interested to see how he'd handle it. I had observed that some people were curious and loved the store, while others occasionally freaked and left in a huff.

My first reaction to my aunt's store was surprise, and, okay I will admit it, delight. My mother had always discouraged anything mystical or what I suppose most people would call 'New-Age' in our home. Even though my father had quietly told me bedtime tales of faeries and the Gods and Goddesses when I was little, he had always kept his personal spiritual beliefs quiet. So I never knew or suspected about his family and their heritage.

After looking around for a moment Duncan started to smile. I had a hunch he wasn't looking at the wares, instead the old oak floor and brick walls were more likely grabbing his attention. When he spotted me behind the card rack, he grinned.

"There you are." He looked all around the store again and focused back on me. "Great looking shop," he said enthusiastically.

"Thanks," I replied as I began to walk to him.

Before I could take more than a few steps, my aunt walked up and moved between the two of us, effectively cutting me off. "Hello. May I help you?" While her tone was polite it was also frosty, very formal, and a bit stiff. It was totally out of character for Gwen.

My stomach tightened in response to the tension suddenly surrounding my aunt and Duncan, which made me wonder if perhaps I *was* a little bit empathic, like Holly. I was sure picking up on emotions today. Seeing auras, feeling tingles from sexy men… it felt like somebody had flipped the switch to high on my sensitivity, but did not bother to tell me.

Out of the corner of my eye, I saw Ivy start to walk forward. She also had a cautious expression on her face. Was she feeling the tension too?

Duncan extended his hand to Aunt Gwen and politely introduced himself. "Hi. I'm Duncan Quinn, I met Autumn this morning. What a great building. Is the exposed brick in here original?"

Aunt Gwen crossed her arms over her chest and ignored his extended hand. "It is."

He gestured at the chunky rustic shelves full of dried herbs, arranged in pretty glass apothecary jars along the back wall of the store. "Do you grow all those herbs in your own gardens?"

"Not all of them," Aunt Gwen told him. I had never seen her so stiff with a customer before.

"My mother studies herbalism," Duncan announced. "I bet she would love your shop." All good will, he started to move towards the back wall, to apparently check out those herbs, when a loud impatient tap sounded on the glass door.

His cousin Julian stood outside the door and gestured with a frown for Duncan to come out. "Let's go!" Julian called.

"In a minute." Unconcerned, Duncan ignored his cousin and went to get a closer look at the herb filled apothecary jars.

There was another loud tap on the glass door. I saw Julian yank his hand back from the glass as if it had burned him. He stepped back from the door, frowned down at his knuckles, and if possible, looked even angrier.

"I mean it Duncan. We need to go!" He sounded really and truly pissed off. "Right now!" He insisted.

"What's his deal?" I asked Ivy quietly as she stepped to my side. "He could come inside the shop and wait."

"No. He can't," said Gwen softly and in a deadly serious tone.

I stood there with my mouth hanging open. I had never seen her act that way before. Power seemed to crackle off of her, and I automatically backed up a step, tugging Ivy with me.

Duncan didn't notice the sudden change in my aunt, or hear what she had said as he was all the way across the sales floor, but I sure did. I swung my gaze from

Aunt Gwen to the guy outside, as Julian backed farther away from the glass door but continued to call for his cousin.

Duncan finally glanced over his shoulder at his cousin, who was looking angrier by the moment while he stood out there shouting on the sidewalk. Duncan rolled his eyes at Julian and then picked up an Enchantments business card off the shop's checkout counter and tucked it in his jeans pocket.

He walked up to Aunt Gwen and then told her that he would come back later. "I'll bring my mother in to shop," he promised.

My aunt said nothing in response.

He smiled at me and headed for the door, calling for his cousin to settle down. As soon as he stepped outside, his cousin grabbed his arm and hauled him off. Ivy and I both went together to the door and watched them leave.

"Real subtle, Julian. What the hell is wrong with you?" Duncan asked.

We could hear Julian as they moved further down the sidewalk, "We are not supposed to cross into the Bishop's territory, and you know it!"

"That's ancient history." Duncan stopped and scowled at his cousin. "It's your problem, not mine."

In a moment, they had disappeared around the corner.

Territory? What the hell did that mean? "Okaaaay," I drew out the word. "That was bizarre."

"All energies not in alignment with me, must now depart." Was Aunt Gwen's reply as she made a broad shooing gesture, and then crossed her arms defensively over her chest.

"Wait, what did you just say?" I asked as I looked back at her.

As an answer, she focused over my head. Which of course made both Ivy and I look up, to see what she was staring at.

"Remind me to re-enchant the wards." Aunt Gwen growled as she stalked forward and peered up at the large, dried, fan-shaped herbal arrangement displayed over the shop's front door. "I am surprised he was even able to get that close to the door," she said.

"Huh?" I asked. *What in the world was going on?*

In answer, Aunt Gwen simply pointed up at the pretty floral swag, hanging right above the shop's door. "That, my girl, is a defensive ward. The dried herbs woven into it are protective and a spell has been worked into the design. It protects the store, wards off negativity, and keeps evil from entering."

"You mean the flowers above the door are a kind of protective spell?" I asked her. I tipped my head up to regard that floral swag more carefully. Come to think of it. there were similar dried floral arrangements above the back door of the shop and over both the main doors at the manor as well.

"And what, it didn't do its job right?" I asked. I still had so much to learn about magick.

As Ivy and I stood there, looking up at the 'ward', all I knew was that I wanted away from it. Especially if it was broken. "So you're saying that Julian Drake is *evil*?" I demanded. Without thinking about what I was doing or why, I put my hand on Ivy's arm and drew her away, out from underneath that large arrangement of dried flowers.

As if on cue, the swag suddenly dropped, and fell hard, as if it weighed hundreds of pounds. It hit the wide planked oak floor of the shop with an impressive thud. The arrangement broke apart on impact, and dried herbs and flowers seem to explode and scatter everywhere when they hit the floor.

Ivy and I both squeaked and jumped back when the floral swag fell. Now we all stood waving our hands in front of our faces, and coughing as the dried herbs floated slowly back down to the oak floor.

"My spidey senses are tingling all over." Ivy said as she looked up to where the floral swag had hung, and then down to where it had burst all over the floor. She shuddered dramatically.

I couldn't help but shudder in reaction as well.

CHAPTER 4

"Well that explains it." Aunt Gwen said in a grim voice as she looked down at what was left of the floral arrangement. "The ward has taken all of the negativity it can, the protective spell is spent."

"I can help you clean it up." I reached down to pick up the bigger pieces of the floral arrangement off the floor.

"No!" Aunt Gwen's sharp reply stopped me in my tracks and I gaped at her. She closed her eyes and took a deep stabilizing breath and seemed to pull herself together. As she exhaled, the serenity I typically associated with my aunt returned to her.

"Don't touch it." She told us, as she reached out and flipped the lock on the door, spinning the door sign over to 'Closed'. "We have work to do," she announced.

"Are we going to do a protection spell, right now?" Ivy asked, practically rubbing her hands together in anticipation. That was new. I had never seen the family do an actual spell together before.

Aunt Gwen looked over at the two of us. "No time like the present." Her tone was gentler, but still serious. "Ivy, I would like you to go and pick out two big chunks of the black tourmaline."

Ivy nodded and hurried to the crystal display and picked out two palm sized pieces of the chunky crystals. Aunt Gwen sent me into the back of the store for a dust pan and her big, hand-made willow broom. When I came back, I found she'd gathered up a black votive candle, a glass candle holder, a bottle of spring water, and a stick of dragon's blood incense from the store's stock. Then she pulled out a big black garbage bag and a container of salt from under the front counter.

Explaining that she wanted the two of us to stay away from the broken floral arrangement, Aunt Gwen took the broom and dustpan from me, and swept up the herbs and the pieces of the floral swag and put them inside of the garbage bag. She handed me her broom when she finished and set the container of salt down on the floor at her side.

She lit the little black votive candle and set it in a glass holder and placed it in the display window to the left of the shop's front door. Gwen lit the incense stick and set that in its holder, in the window on the other side of the door. Next, she opened the bottle of water and poured a bit into the palm of her hand. She sprinkled the water lightly on the now clean floor and around the doorway.

With her wet fingers she drew a pentagram in the center of the wide old wooden doorframe— right above the shop's front door. As she finished, she shook her hands briskly and droplets scattered to the floor. As the drops fell Gwen said, "By the powers of air, fire and water, I cleanse this space."

As the words were spoken, I felt something shift in the store. The mood felt lighter somehow and the overhead lights seemed to grow a little brighter. I looked suspiciously up at the lights, as Gwen directed Ivy to place the crystals on the floor, one on either side of the closed and locked door. Lastly, she had Ivy pour a thin line of salt across the threshold. Salt was not only protective, Aunt Gwen quietly informed me, but also evil could not pass a barrier of salt.

She continued her ritual by saying, "By the power of the element of earth, I protect this space. No evil can enter here, no manipulation can find its way in to do harm. The elements four now weave together, as I speak this charm." She stepped back and took both Ivy and I by the hand. "As I will it…" She began.

"So shall it be," Ivy and Gwen said together.

"So shall it be." I repeated after my aunt and cousin. I guessed it was the right thing to do as they both beamed at me.

"Ivy," Gwen then asked her daughter, "would you please cleanse the broom?"

Ivy retrieved the broom, and held up the bristle part of the broom over the incense smoke that was streaming up from the holder. Ivy looked at me and explained, "Passing an item through incense smoke is a quick way to cleanse it. Plus dragon's blood is a protective scent."

As I watched the fragrant smoke roll around the broom's bristles, Ivy continued with, "By the powers of air, I cleanse this broom. All negativity must depart."

I looked over at my aunt, and she nodded. She seemed pleased with my attention.

"That should hold us for now," She told the two of us. "I'm going to dispose of these dried flowers and I think we will close up a bit early for the day." She sent Ivy to the register and asked her to start running the daily reports so we could close out.

I went around the shop and clicked off the music and, with direction from Ivy, clicked off the various overhead lights. I picked up the forgotten greeting cards and set them neatly aside to be dealt with tomorrow. There was really no need to straighten, as we had been organizing and cleaning to help with end-of-summer inventory. So closing up the shop went very quickly.

By the time we had finished with the closing paperwork, the incense stick had burned itself out. Aunt Gwen picked up the burning candle and placed it, in its holder, inside of the shop's bathroom sink. Where she told me it could continue to burn safely even while we were gone. But at the rate the candle was burning, I didn't think it would take very long.

I nudged Ivy as we gathered up our belongings, and

asked, "Why is the candle burning out so quickly? That's strange isn't it?"

Ivy looked back at the candle and its dancing flame and shrugged. "No, not always. A fast burning candle means the magick is either working really quickly or that there is a lot of energy working against the spell."

Well there's a happy thought.

I was on the verge of asking questions, when Gwen gestured for us to go out the shop's back door before her. "We will talk about this more at home." She announced.

As the three of us headed out the back door, Aunt Gwen hauled the black garbage bag with her. I locked the rear door, while she walked across the back parking lot to the dumpster. I could hear her chanting low as she opened up the bag and looked down at the remnants of the floral swag. Then for good measure she pulled that container of salt out of her purse, where she had apparently stashed it, opened up the container and dumped all the remaining salt over the broken dried flowers inside the garbage bag.

She knotted the bag three times and chucked it into the dumpster followed by the empty carton of salt. Ivy and I watched this before we climbed into the back seat of my aunt's car.

I elbowed Ivy. "So would you call this an average day at the shop... Exploding wards, flickering lights, and protection spells?"

"Nah. This is a better day than most."

I seriously hoped she was kidding me.

As we pulled out of the parking lot a moment later, Gwen looked back at Ivy and I. "Girls we need to stop at the grocery store on our way home. I need to stock up on a few things."

"Salt?" Ivy and I asked at the same time.

In response, Aunt Gwen flashed us a fierce grin in the review mirror.

***

I resisted the urge to bombard my aunt with questions on the drive home. It wasn't easy. We stopped at the grocery store and I was almost disappointed to see that she picked up some fresh fruit, a gallon of milk, garlic, lemons, and a couple of containers of salt. Hardly what one would consider witchy items. But with my aunt... you just never knew. Magickal items, as I was starting to learn, could be anything.

Ivy had been texting from the moment we got in the car and I had a feeling she was updating Holly on the day's events. Different, though they might be, they were fiercely loyal to one another. When Holly finished her shift at the pool today and checked her messages she'd be up to speed with the day's happenings.

When we arrived back at the manor, I hauled the bags in and dumped them on the kitchen table. Aunt Gwen and Ivy followed me into the kitchen, and Ivy announced that she had a message from Holly. It seemed the country club pool would be open later tonight, and she was able to get a few passes. If we wanted, Ivy and I could come up to the pool and swim for free until closing

There was also a message on the answering machine for Aunt Gwen from one of her coven-sisters. I tucked the milk in the fridge and waited until she had finished listening to the message.

"If you girls want to go to the pool tonight, that's fine with me," she announced.

"What about what happened at the store today? You said we would talk about that at home," I reminded her.

"We will," she assured me. "But I would like all four of you to be here when we do," she said, meaning Bran as well. "I could drop you off at the country club, and then you could ride home with Holly when her shift is over at seven."

I tried to decide whether I should use this opportunity to have some alone time with my aunt so I could discuss my dreams and the other events of the day, or if I should go to the pool and relax with my young cousins. But the lure of lying around poolside and swimming on one of the last days of summer was simply too much to resist. Besides if the three of us were alone, we could privately discuss what had happened today. I really wanted Holly's impressions on everything.

"That's okay, I can drive my truck." I volunteered.

"Sweet!" Ivy gave a fist pump. "I'm gonna go get

my stuff together." Ivy clattered up the kitchen stairs.

A half hour later, we arrived at the club, me in a bright green swimsuit and aqua sarong—as color coordinated as I ever got — and Ivy in all black as usual: a black mesh cover-up over her—wait for it— black bikini. At least she had switched out the boots for flip-flops.

We hustled to the few empty chaise lounge chairs, poolside, spread out our towels, and settled in. Holly was easy enough to spot perched up high in her life guard stand at the side of the lap pool. She gave us a wave and went back to her duties.

It was a hot and steamy late afternoon, and a few minutes later, Ivy and I dove in the lap pool to cool off. We swam around for a while, me with laps and Ivy just swimming or floating hither and yon. After we climbed out, we smeared on the sunscreen, and got down to the serious business of getting some sun, while we still could. I combed out my wet hair and Ivy offered to braid it for me so I handed her a hair tie and turned around.

"Your hair is so thick." Ivy muttered as she tamed it into a braid.

"I get tempted to whack it shorter every summer." I admitted.

"Don't do that. It goes all the way down your back, and I love the color." Ivy finished up the braid and patted my shoulder to signal that she was done.

I looked over my shoulder at Ivy, "It's only light

brown, not very exciting."

"If my hair was that color, I wouldn't dye it."

"Which reminds me, what is your natural hair color?" I asked her, as I eyeballed my cousin's black hair.

That made Ivy laugh and we decided, after a brief discussion, to get a sandwich or something for dinner, later at the club. It was nice to feel like a beach bum, hanging at the pool, listening to the music played over the loud speakers, and enjoying the last days of summer.

I had flipped over to my back and was rearranging my chaise to a more upright position, as Ivy made some snarky comments about a few of the young women parading about in bikinis directly across the pool. I started to laugh and I sat up, adjusting my prescription sunglasses, and tried to get a better look at the pack of females in question.

A lone man lounged under a shaded patio, where several other couples wearing tennis whites sat enjoying drinks. He seemed gym buff and was wearing mirrored aviator shades, swim trunks, and an open shirt. A second man, more casually dressed in khaki shorts and a shirt, walked over and joined the group. He was facing away from us, but the women were all hanging around both men and it was like a scene from a reality TV show. As if in agreement the song playing changed to 'It's Not About the Money'. How ironic.

I laughed to myself and dismissed the group. As I

chuckled with Ivy about the song being played over the speakers, I saw the gym dude stare over at us and point to his blonde companion. I figured he was probably checking out Ivy in her little black bikini. If he thought he could juggle multiple girls and Ivy at the same time... the guy was delusional. Ivy would shred him up with a few choice words and smile while she did so.

Unimpressed with their swarming ladies and the guy ogling my cousin, I leaned back and closed my eyes behind my sunglasses, leaving them to it. I was so relaxed. I hummed along with the music and sighed. Feeling blissfully stress-free for the first time in weeks, I relaxed and let my mind wander.

I started to anyway... but then in my mind's eye I saw a fuzzy scene unfold.

Holly sat in her stand high above the water, calmly watching the many swimmers in the pool. Abruptly she stood up in her lifeguard chair and studied the pool intently. Suddenly, Holly chucked her sunglasses, blew her whistle loud and long, and jumped in feet first, holding a long, flat, orange flotation device.

Crazily the images shifted and I saw a man smile and laugh in satisfaction, but other than his expression I couldn't see him clearly. Then I saw a woman in too much gold and diamond jewelry with a cell phone. She was screaming at the edge of the pool clutching her cell phone, but not jumping in.

Then all I saw was water. Everywhere. It crushed painfully down and suffocated me.

With a start, I sat up and pressed my hand to my galloping heart. Ivy, having seen me jerk upright, sat up as well and reached for me. "What's wrong?" She asked quietly.

I looked around the pool and saw nothing out of the ordinary. No dramas, and there were no big rescues in progress. I gagged and coughed.

"Crap." I tried to breathe. I thumped my fist against my heart. My chest was so tight it felt like I was having an anxiety attack. "A damn vision," I said to Ivy. I tried to calm down, but I could hardly catch my breath. *What was with me today?*

"What did you see?"

"Holly jumping in after a swimmer, some guy laughing about it, and a woman in too much jewelry screaming at her." I gripped the sides of the chaise lounge and panted, breathing way too quickly. "Water. Water everywhere."

"You are going to hyperventilate," Ivy quietly warned me. "Autumn, try and slow your breathing down."

I really did try to slow my breathing down, but couldn't. If anything my chest felt tighter. I *knew* something big was about to happen. "It's going to happen soon," I said quietly to Ivy.

What should I do? Should I try and warn Holly? Should I go stand watch at the side of the pool myself? Or should I simply put my head between my knees and try and not pass out?

It ended up I didn't have to try and decide what to do. As I looked up at Ivy, I could see Holly high in her lifeguard chair off to our right. I watched unsurprised and a little numb as she suddenly stood up in her chair with her whistle in her mouth.

Like in the vision I had just experienced, Holly stood for a second. Then she tossed her sunglasses, blew loud and long and vaulted off that chair, jumping way out and into the deep end of the lap pool, feet first.

Both Ivy and I had jumped to our feet after Holly went in to the water, and I didn't see anybody struggling. So I knew whoever she went in after, was well under. I clutched Ivy's hand. For the first time, I realized that Holly's summer job was actually dangerous. Another life guard jumped in a second later. For a moment the pool fell silent. Then pandemonium ensued.

As we watched, Holly surfaced with a child in her arms. As she turned in the water, the movement had the child leaning back against her, and using the floatation device to help hold his head above water, Holly sped over to the edge of the pool.

To the left of our pool chairs, a woman in a trim two-piece stood poolside chatting on a cell phone. And as I had *seen*, she had on way too much jewelry and her hair was perfect. She obviously had not come to the pool to swim. The woman chatted away, and moved, out of curiosity, closer to the edge of the pool to see the goings on.

The second lifeguard helped Holly lift the child out of the water. Together, they laid him down on the edge of the pool deck. The little boy looked to be about five years old and he was very still. Too still, I realized as my heart sunk.

Then the jewelry-laden cell phone woman started to scream. The rescued boy was her son.

A pool employee rushed to call emergency services, while a few more people tried to keep the hysterical mother out of the lifeguard's way.

They began to work on the boy and a few seconds later he started to gag.

Holly and the other life guard rolled the boy over on his side, to encourage him to cough up more water. The little boy tried to sit up but Holly kept him lying down. She leaned over him and spoke to him and he calmed down a bit.

Knowing there was nothing we could do; Ivy and I backed up and went over to sit in our pool chairs. Ivy guided me over, and I admit that I fell into my chaise lounge more than I sat back down. I had never had a waking vision come on me, and then play out so *quickly*, ever before. Shaken, I put my head in my hands, pushed my own sunglasses up on my head, and tried to focus while Ivy kept telling me to breathe.

I jolted when a large, warm hand settled on my back. I felt a zip of energy and looked up to see Duncan Quinn leaning over my shoulder with a concerned expression on his face.

"Autumn, are you okay?" He asked me quietly.

"Just dandy," I snapped and put my head back in my hands. Humiliation and nausea surged through me. I would not throw up. I told my churning stomach. I would not.

"I'm going to get you something to drink, Autumn. Sit, and try and breathe." Ivy ordered me. Then as I lifted my head a bit, to frown at her for being so bossy, I watched as she leveled a serious look at Duncan. "Be useful and stay with her until I get back."

"I will," he said, then took Ivy's chaise. We sat quietly for a few seconds directly across from one another. "I saw you from across the pool and was coming over to talk to you," Duncan told me.

Perfect. He had been one of the men all those women were drooling over. *It figured.* I stayed silent and concentrated on not barfing all over his sandaled feet, which I was currently looking at.

"I saw you jerk up in your chair," he said.

I lifted my head slowly and watched him steadily. Even slightly out of focus, his blonde hair looked great in the breeze. He looked so cool and casual in his pressed khaki shorts and polo shirt. Now that he was sitting across from me I noticed a neat tribal design tattoo that wrapped around his right bicep. I gulped.

With the way he sat, the sun created a halo of light around him. I thought that it looked like his aura, all golden and sparkling. *Damn it, not again!*

I continued to watch him carefully and then slowly

blinked a couple of times. To my relief, the image of him having an aura faded away.

He returned my careful look with one of his own and continued by saying, "I overheard what you said to your cousin about having a vision. I saw how it affected you."

My heart slammed painfully, and I broke a sweat. "So?" I glared at him and managed to raise an eyebrow. I was proud of that look. Kind of haughty, kind of cool and belligerent... I hoped it would work. I was so *not* having this conversation with a man that I had just met.

"It happened exactly like you said it would."

Apparently I was. "I'm going to have to repeat myself. So?"

He smirked at my tone. "Does this foreseeing the future thing happen often with you?" He asked me so calmly that it was unnerving.

I stared at him, and felt heat rising in my face. I started to say something really rude but he cut me off.

"Here comes your cousin. Why don't you sit still for a minute and ground and center yourself."

"Huh?" Had he told me to ground and center? As in ground and center my energy so I could become calm and focused? That was a *magickal* term. Ivy and Holly had been trying to teach me to ground and center for the past few days.

Holy crap was he a Witch too? I reached for my glasses and put them back on my nose. Maybe they would help guard my expression. But I didn't know what the point was. He didn't even seem fazed by overhearing me talking about a vision, or by what had happened.

Ivy shoved a soda at me. "Drink it," she ordered.

I took a sip and made a face. "Bleh! That's not a diet soda." I cringed at the sugary taste.

"Drink it anyway. The sugar will help with the psychic distress," Duncan advised calmly. Then he greeted Ivy as I sat there with my mouth hanging open. "Hi Ivy, nice to see you again."

Confidently, Ivy sat right down next to him on the chaise. "He's right. The sugar will help you feel better." Then she tipped down her sunglasses and shot him a look. "So, what do you want, Duncan?"

"To help, if I can," he answered.

This was all way too other-worldly for me. I decided that my best course of action was to do as they suggested and drink the sugary soda and to ground myself.

As we watched, the EMS team and a police officer showed up. They took the little boy and his still hysterical mother off to a waiting ambulance. Holly stood and was giving the pool manager and officer a report on what had happened while a different lifeguard came and took over Holly's post.

The pool slowly went back to normal and Duncan was apparently in no hurry to leave us. I started to wonder at his ease at sitting thigh-to-thigh with my cousin. My gothic, gorgeous teenage cousin wearing a big silver pentagram necklace and a little black bikini.

As we watched, Holly excused herself from speaking to the manager and the police, and walked over to us. She nodded at Duncan politely before she spoke to us. "I'll have to fill out a report but I'll be done in a little while. The boy should be fine once he coughs up all the water. They are taking him in as a precaution." She told us and then she asked us to wait for her.

Ivy and I promised that we would wait, and Holly went off with her boss. This left my cousin and me with Mr. Tall, Blonde, and Mysterious, as I sat and sipped my soda slowly. The sugar did help. Like Duncan had said it would.

And how exactly, did Duncan know about the 'psychic distress' thing, and grounding and centering anyway? Did everyone in this town know magick, except me? It was a little mortifying.

I looked over at him where he still sat chatting with Ivy. About, if you can believe it, the tattoo on his arm! Ivy wanted a tattoo in a big way. Apparently, she figured he'd have insider information on getting inked. Too bizarre. Would it blow my image, or add to it, if Ivy found out that I had a little crescent moon and stars tattooed high on my left hip?

I set the soda down and squared my shoulders. Time for some answers. "Okay Duncan," I began, "explain to me how you know about psychic distress and grounding and centering."

"Probably the same way that you do," he said quietly.

"Autumn," Ivy said and, her serious tone surprised me. "Take a good look at the design on his arm."

Duncan twisted his arm towards me and I reached to brush the shirt sleeve up and out of the way, to better see the ink on his bicep. I could see it very clearly now with my glasses on. I ignored the little stomach flip and tingle of energy that I felt.

It was then that I noticed the design was not simply a tribal tattoo as I had originally thought. The pattern of the knot work was actually two intertwined dragons. Finally, almost hidden at the center of the design, between the dragon's tails was small, upright pentagram.

"So, you *are* a Witch." I said mostly to myself.

"It's a family tradition." He confirmed.

I sat there stunned.

"What?" He asked me with a quiet laugh. "Did you think yours was the only family in town with a legacy of magick?"

CHAPTER 5

A few hours later, I drove home from the country club following Ivy and Holly in my old pickup truck. I could see as I followed behind them that the twins were chatting away. I took a deep breath in and let it out slowly, trying to relax. As far as days went, it had been fairly intense and I was wiped out.

Recalling Duncan's announcement about his own family, I really had not known what to say to him. He had only smiled at me and looked serious. Ivy, for once, was silent and had nothing sarcastic to add. The three of us sat there awkwardly. Finally, Duncan stood up, and said quietly that he would talk to me later. When he walked away, I did not call him back.

Holly arrived right after Duncan left, so we grabbed sandwiches from the concession stand at the club, some sodas, and a couple of bags of chips. The three of us found a cool, quiet, shady spot in the concession area where we brought Holly up to speed on the day's events.

I told them about meeting Duncan, the energy jolts I felt when we touched, seeing auras, and the vision at the pool. I wanted their opinion on why all of this was happening to me today.

Ivy leaned forward. "I think you are coming into a new level of power. You don't have to hide your magick or your psychic abilities anymore. So now it's like they can finally come out and play."

Not sure I believed her; I sat there and said nothing.

Ivy smirked at me and tossed a chip to a hovering sparrow. "Wait and see."

"She's only been here a few weeks. She's had a lot to take in." Holly, on the other hand, was more sympathetic. She quietly held out her hand with a few chip crumbs in it, and a brave little sparrow flew in, grabbed the biggest piece, and flew off again. "Besides, I think her running into Duncan Quinn so many times in one day is very interesting." Holly grinned at me and wiggled her eyebrows.

"Oh yeah. He of the hot tattoos, and dark, dangerous family..." Ivy said.

"Dark and dangerous family? What's that supposed to mean?" I frowned at Ivy.

"You'll find out." She predicted.

A few more birds gathered on our tabletop, trying to work their way over to Holly's hand to get more crumbs. She obliged them and they flew away chirping and happy. After a few more moments, we all decided unanimously to head back to the manor.

I snapped back to the present time as we pulled our cars into the driveway and the big iron gate closed automatically behind us. I assumed there was a remote control for the gate, but, honestly, at this point I wasn't sure anymore. We all climbed out and stood in the driveway, looking up at the house.

At sunset, the house and the gardens were even more spectacular, almost mysterious. A thin waxing moon hung low in the western sky. The landscape lighting came on and the stars started to peep out. Looking up at the pointed towers of the manor, I felt like more of an outsider than ever. That house held secrets, and so did my father's family. What weren't they telling me?

I cleared my throat. "I have a hunch that there is more going on about our family than you have all told me."

Ivy said nothing, and Holly put her arm around her twin.

"Your mother has been wonderful to me," I said. "But I had the weirdest feeling this morning, before we left for the store, that she was hiding something or trying to distract me."

"Well, standing out here in the driveway is not going to get you any answers." Holly said. Let's go in."

Ivy raised an eyebrow at me as if in challenge, and we all started towards the house, together.

Ivy opened the door and, as I entered, I saw the usual floral swag that hung over the inside potting room door was missing. I dumped our pool bags on the work table and pointed up. "The herbal swag is gone." All that was there now was an empty nail.

"That was a ward too. Like mom had at the shop." Ivy said.

"Yes." Holly's voice sounded solemn. She touched my arm and gestured for me to stay put with Ivy.

Holly walked to the opening of the family room. She raised her arms up, palms out as if she was feeling for something. I felt the hair rise up on the back of my neck. She turned in a slow circle; the low light from the lamp burning in the room made her hair seem to glow. After a moment Holly stopped and lowered her arms. She looked over at us and whispered, "The house feels different. It feels... tight."

"Tight?" I stared at my cousin, "Do I even want to know what that means?"

"Like the energy of the house has been pulled in closer towards the center of the house." Holly gestured with her hands, pulling her palms closer together as she spoke.

"Let's find your mom," I suggested.

The three of us started out of the family room; Holly poked her head in the downstairs bedroom Gwen used as an office, and then into the kitchen, while Ivy went upstairs. I moved from the entryway, into the living room, and finally checked the dining room. Since all were empty of people, Holly and I went to the front landing and the main stairs.

Ivy jogged back down the main staircase, and blew

out an aggravated breath. "Where do you suppose she is?"

Holly stopped dead, cocked her head to the side and announced. "Mom's upstairs in the attic."

"But we only use that for storage. Why would she be up there? " Ivy looked up the stairs.

I didn't even question it. Holly clearly sensed Aunt Gwen's location in the house in the same way she'd felt the energy of the house had changed. We started up the stairs together.

We found Aunt Gwen coming out of a door on the second floor, a door that I'd taken as a closet. I saw steep steps behind her, before she shut the door. "Girls." She opened her arms and pulled all three of us close.

"What's wrong?" I asked from the middle of the hug.

Aunt Gwen reached out and cupped Holly's face in her hands. "I'm so proud of you. I heard about the big rescue at the pool today."

"That was fast," Holly said under her breath.

"My network of information is pretty extensive. Go change out of your suits and come to my room." She held up a hand to cut all of us off from asking any questions. "Quickly. We need to talk."

I headed for my room and stepped over a remaining box I'd yet to unpack. I peeled out of my dry swim suit. I pulled my hair loose from the long braid I had used at the pool, and tossed on the same clothes I had worn to the shop that day. I swapped out my sunglasses for my regular glasses then caught my reflection in the dresser mirror. My green eyes seemed way too large in my oval face. Even though I had gotten a little sun up at the pool, my black t-shirt made me appear pale. Running a brush through my damp hair I reminded myself that I had had an *intense* day. Those two precognitive visions: one of Bran and the other of the boy up at the pool. Seeing auras... Maybe Ivy's remark about me coming into a new level of power wasn't too far off the mark after all. Wanting answers more than ever, I headed barefoot up to the front of the house where the master bedroom was, with its spacious sitting area inside of the turret.

The circular, turret area was what Aunt Gwen used as a ritual room. The entire bedroom/ turret room had shiny old oak floors. While the turret area boasted curvy walls and a half circle window seat.

"This has been one crazy day." I said to Gwen and went to sit on the padded blue window seat cushion.

Gwen returned a few books to a wooden bookshelf that ranged along one side of the room. "It certainly has."

On the marble topped table, that my cousins had informed me was used as a magickal workspace and an altar, there were three new floral swags. A large basket filled with dried herbs, ribbon, and floral wire was on the floor next to the table.

"Conjured up some new floral wards, while we were at the pool?" I asked.

Gwen nodded, and Holly and Ivy entered in the room and both headed for the comfy loveseat slip-covered in pale yellow. They tended to stick together; I suppose it was a twin thing. Holly had taken her hair out of its neat ponytail and it sprang in wild red-blonde curls down the back of her plain pink tank top.

Ivy had brushed her hair back, off her face, and twisted it into a clip. She had tossed on an oversized black t-shirt and shorts.

I wondered about Bran. Was his excellency going to join us this evening? "Where's Bran?" I almost hated to ask.

"On his way." Aunt Gwen answered.

Merlin streaked into the room and jumped up to join me. He sat up like a little Egyptian statue of a temple cat. He held himself very regal and still.

"I hope you girls all know how much I love you," Aunt Gwen said to her daughters. She paused for a moment, as if searching for the right words, "All of your life I have taught you the old ways. I watched with pride as you each embraced your gifts. I taught you both the joys and responsibilities of the Craft and its ethics... but shielded you from some of the more difficult aspects of our legacy. And in my effort to protect you I have been remiss."

Ivy and Holly shifted together on the loveseat and held hands.

Gwen faced me. "Autumn, you are my brother's child. I love you too. I'm so happy to have you here with us again. You may not remember, but you lived in this house for your first years before your parents went out east."

That was news to me, "I had no idea. Why did they leave?" I asked.

"When Arthur married your mother, he wished only for a normal life. By the time you were two years old there were problems in their marriage and your mother was very unhappy living here. So your father moved you, and your mother, to the east coast and started a new life."

"That was why we never came back here for a visit." I guessed.

"It was one of the reasons." Gwen continued, "Your father started his landscaping business and raised you well away from us and the legacy that we share. So you were brought up not understanding exactly what it is that you have inside of you. That was his choice, and while I may not approve of what he did, he was my little brother and I loved him all the same."

My mind raced as I considered what I had just been told.

Gwen interrupted my thoughts as she said, "Now you have come back to us. You are a powerful young woman with no idea of what you are capable of or how to protect yourself from those who may try to exploit your gift."

"What do you mean, exactly?"

"I should have explained that for every light there is

also a shadow." She looked at each of us, deliberately. "When you came to live with us, I never imagined that we would find ourselves having any sort of contact with the Drake family." Aunt Gwen said softly.

"What does that have to do with anything?" I frowned at her. For comfort, I stroked Merlin's long back. He leaned into the petting, but otherwise stayed alert and watchful.

Aunt Gwen sighed. "Magick, like nature, is a neutral force. I have taught my children to work magick ethically and to not interfere with the free will of others."

"You've talked to us about neutrality before, Mom." Ivy said. "I explained to Autumn the other day that we have to cast spells from a calm and centered place, that we do *not* manipulate other people with our magick, and we don't cast in anger."

Holly nodded, her curly hair bouncing. "It was one of the first lessons you taught us Mom. Why are you worried about this now?"

"Because, girls, there are families that follow a different type of magickal tradition, less earth centered and more ceremonial. Not the natural magick we work with. However, this is not merely a difference in styles or taste..."

Aunt Gwen stopped and seemed to be choosing her next words with care. "The fact is that not all magick is positive or constructive. Some individuals use magick to control, to coerce, and to harm," she paused and then looked straight at me. "And there are those that even specialize in the darker magicks."

I heard footsteps in the hall and Bran poked his head into the room. On cue, Merlin arched his back and hissed at the intrusion. "Mom?" Bran reached for Gwen. "I got the text message. What's happened?" To my surprise Bran was as casually dressed as I had ever seen him. Gone was the jacket and conservative tie. While his dark dress slacks still looked neat and professional, his pale blue dress shirt was unbuttoned at the throat, and I saw, as he came into the room and took his mother's hands, that he had his shirt sleeves folded up. It boggled my mind a bit. Bran looked almost like a regular man and not a stuffy academic.

Aunt Gwen smiled at her son. "Take a seat Bran and I will bring you up to speed. Also, I am going to tell Autumn some of our the family history. You should be here for this."

Bran nodded, and started towards the window seat to sit next me. Then he stopped and reconsidered as Merlin continued to hiss and let out a warning wail. "Call him off." He ordered me.

I resisted the urge to say "Good kitty," and pat Merlin on the head. As if he knew my thoughts, Merlin whipped his head around to glare at me. Instead I said to Bran, "He's your family's cat. I can't help it if he doesn't like you. " I shrugged.

As Bran walked towards me, Merlin narrowed his eyes at my cousin with an impressive growl. Holly gasped and covered her mouth with her hands, while Ivy sat there next to her sister on the couch, grinning at the cat. I have to admit I had never seen Merlin act so aggressively. Bran stopped again and seemed to reconsider as Merlin cranked up the growl to a yowl.

"Oh for Goddess sake!" Aunt Gwen rolled her eyes and marched across the room to face down a mass of protective, spitting black fur.

"Merlin!" Aunt Gwen snapped her fingers under the cat's nose and he cocked his head up to look at Gwen. "Behave yourself or leave the room!" She pointed at the doorway and Merlin's growling noises turned off like a light switch. Merlin sat there and blinked innocently up at my aunt. Then he laid down next to me on the window seat, stretched out on his belly, and let out a cute little meow. It sounded so ridiculous after the hissing and spitting that I chuckled.

Aunt Gwen waved Bran to the window seat. "Now, sit down next to Autumn." She directed him.

"I'll grab a chair," Bran stated.

"Nonsense," Aunt Gwen snapped back.

Slowly, as if approaching a cobra, Bran walked up and sat down next to me in the empty spot on the window seat. He did not take his eyes off Merlin until he was fully seated. Merlin laid his head down on his white tipped paws, and began to purr, looking adorable —just for spite, I'm sure.

"That cat is so twisted," Bran complained.

Bran's comment had Merlin looking up at him.

Merlin rose and climbed up to circle and then sprawled himself half way across my cousin's lap, who did his best not to react. Merlin rarely bothered with Bran. He tried to nudge the cat off his lap, but the cat snuggled up as if they were the best of friends. Fifteen pounds of cat pinned Bran to his spot. He wasn't going anywhere.

Merlin draped over Bran's lap and stretched one white paw out and over towards me. It rested on my arm as if he was letting me know. I was still his favorite, even though he was enjoying making my cousin squirm.

Bran stared at me as if it were my fault, grumbling about cat hair being all over his new pants. I smiled at him very sweetly. Aunt Gwen shut her eyes and muttered something about patience being a virtue.

"Mom, you were mentioning people who specialized in dark magicks?" Holly said, apparently trying to pull things back on track.

"Yes, I was," Gwen's voice was as grim as I had ever heard it, even after her confrontation with a Drake in her shop.

"Know this," she began. "There are those individuals who manipulate and abuse the Craft and the powers of magick for their own gain. They care nothing about the harm they cause, or the free will of others. The Bishops, and other families, have stood against this type of abuse of the power for generations. Because of this we have made enemies."

Bran took over the story at this point, "According to

our family history, a feud began in the 1700's after our ancestors left the village of Salem and moved north. Three other families with the Bishops began a new community. These four families settled quietly, planted their crops, and raised their children in peace. Eventually the families became combined as there were marriages from one family into another. Then the settlement grew and, eventually, the territory that the four families had first settled became part of the state of New Hampshire."

New Hampshire, I thought with a jolt. Where I had grown up and lived with Mom and Dad before he passed away. "How do you know all of this?" I asked my cousin.

"Bran is the family historian." Aunt Gwen said. "He is our record keeper."

"Sort of like a magickal librarian?" I asked.

"Yes, but he not only keeps our ancestor's journals and grimoires, he has studied them. He also knows the history and has worked on the genealogy of the four families." Gwen explained.

"Autumn, if it helps, think of him like Giles from *Buffy the Vampire Slayer*," Ivy grinned.

Bran rolled his eyes and let out a long suffering sigh at Ivy's characterization of him. I guess he didn't like being compared to the slightly stuffy, tweed wearing, English, librarian.

I gestured towards the bookcase across the room filled with modern and colorful books on the Craft.

"I've seen shelves with magickal books here and in the family room, but these books are not as old as what you are talking about."

Holly leaned forward on the loveseat towards me. "Autumn, there is a separate library filled with antique books and magickal journals secreted in the house." she said to me.

Bran shifted beside me on the window seat.

"You kept them hidden from me?" I asked.

"Not hidden," Gwen said as if offended. "Private. We keep them private and safe from the people that are not meant to see them."

That hurt, more than I expected, and made me angry. "So you didn't trust me," I said flatly and watched my aunt to see her reaction.

"I am sorrier than I can say that your feelings are hurt. I was trying to protect you and give you some time to adjust to living here, with us, at the manor. But after today, that's all changed."

She looked sincere, but too many extraordinary things had happened today for me to take what she said at face value. When Aunt Gwen asked Bran to finish his story, I sighed loudly.

Bran nodded to his mother and continued. "It was after New Hampshire achieved statehood that a new and powerful family came to the area from the old country. This family was welcomed by the four magickal families at first. Then it became obvious that the magick of the new family was not the gentle folk magick that the original four families had practiced."

He tried to shift Merlin carefully off his lap as he spoke, but the cat continued to sprawl there, ignoring him. "The new family had influence and money; they combined this with their darker magicks. Little by little, they took over the settlement and the surrounding territory. The four families banded together and tried to put a stop to the troubles, but they were not entirely successful."

"Wait." I said. "Are we talking about a war?"

"More like a magickal feud than a war." Gwen explained. "It went on for some time, and then things got complicated between one of our ancestors and the son of the family of dark magicians."

"A Romeo and Juliet type of deal?" I asked.

"A Bishop woman named Patience and a son from the feuding family, James, fell in love. Their relationship angered both of the couple's families. Since both families were against the match, the couple ran off and were married in secret. But even then they could not keep their secret forever." Bran told me.

"Don't tell me, let me guess. She was pregnant." I rolled my eyes. Seriously? This was getting ridiculous. Like some colonial soap opera.

"Yes," Bran nodded, my sarcasm clearly skipping right over his head. "This upset the family of dark magicians so much that they disinherited their son. He, in turn, abjured his magick, never practicing again. He and his bride built a home on Bishop land and waited for their child to be born."

"This couple's story did not have a happy ending," Holly said with a sad face.

"No, it didn't," Bran agreed. "Shortly after their daughter was born, influenza hit the territory. Many people died. The Bishops nursed their family and friends through the epidemic with their herbal remedies as best they could. However, James caught influenza and couldn't be saved. While Patience buried her husband, his family began publicly accusing Patience of witchcraft."

"Which would have been a death sentence back then." Ivy said. "That's even if she survived prison and went on to a trial…" She shuddered.

"That's a little hypocritical, isn't it?" I asked. "Especially since they were supposed to have practiced magick themselves. Wouldn't that have been a stupid thing to start rumors about?"

My aunt nodded in agreement.

"So, what happened to Patience?" I wanted to know, despite myself.

"One night a mob came for Patience, planning to seize her and to take her child." Bran said. "The Bishops and many of their friends tried to stop the mob from storming Patience's cottage, but eventually they broke in. To everyone's shock, Patience and her baby had disappeared. No one, not even her own family, knew where she and her child were. There was a search, but they were never found. Foul play was suspected and no one in the village ever heard from Patience or her child again."

My aunt stepped forward to add, "So a feud began in earnest between the two families, and as the years have passed the feud has continued."

Fascinating. Melodramatic — but fascinating. "So what does this have to do with me?" I demanded.

Bran looked at his mother, who nodded her approval to finish the story. "The last name of the family of dark magicians, James' family... was Drake."

CHAPTER 6

It took a moment for that to sink in. "Seriously?" I laughed at Bran. "You seriously expect me to believe that a family feud between the Drake family and ours — that you say started in colonial America — has held for over three hundred years?" I rolled my eyes at Bran. What a freaking drama queen.

"Eventually new branches of the Bishop family tree and some of the other members of the four families, moved west with the Louisiana Purchase." Bran said. "They came to be settled here, in William's Ford."

Aunt Gwen took up the story. "William's Ford is a unique geographical area as two of the largest rivers on the continent meet here. This is a natural place of power and the families became established permanently. As time passed the Drake family, also drawn by the magick and power of the land, settled here as well."

"And what? The magickal feud continued?" I rubbed my forehead.

"It has. But it's not as overt as it was in the old

days." Aunt Gwen explained.

"I'm going to get a massive headache if you guys keep this history lesson up too much longer." I joked.

To my surprise Holly shook her head at me and Ivy sat there with her fingers steepled. She tapped them together and arched an eyebrow. I was the only person who thought this was funny, apparently.

"I should have known you wouldn't take this seriously." Bran sniffed at me.

I really started to laugh then. "All we need is some melodramatic background music, like the old *Dark Shadows* reruns Dad used to watch."

Aunt Gwen spoke over my laughter. "Regardless, that is how the magickal feud began. It followed the families even as they settled into new territories further west, and it has continued to this day."

"Yeah, clashes of good magick and evil magick pop up in the Midwest every day." I shot back. I was *so* done with this conversation. It had been a hell of a day, and now this nonsense. I was exhausted. I stood up to leave and go back to my room.

"Autumn," my aunt said softly, "I want you to stay away from Duncan Quinn."

"What? Why should I?" I stared at her.

"His family is powerful and not to be underestimated," was her reply.

I stopped and thought about that comment Duncan had made to me today at the club pool, how we were not the only family in town that had magick. That suddenly seemed a little ominous. On the other hand, I considered the jolt and the warm tingly energy I felt whenever we touched. Then, I thought about how much I was attracted to him.

Decision made.

"I will not. This is *your* stupid feud not mine. Besides, you talked to him yourself at the shop today. Duncan is a nice guy." I defended him.

"He was *inside* our shop?" Bran asked incredulously. He stood up and Merlin jumped off his lap with a yowl.

"He walked right over the threshold, introduced himself, and attempted to shake my hand," Gwen said to Bran.

"He was able to comfortably cross the threshold?" Bran asked her.

"He looked comfortable enough to me while he flirted with Autumn," Ivy interjected as she stood at my side.

I thought back to Duncan perusing the shop's herbs. "But, he promised to bring his mother back to shop." I said to my aunt, feeling even more confused. I turned to Bran next. "Duncan said that he knew you, that you helped him with old blueprints and historical records of the buildings he was rehabbing." I don't know why I even bothered, Bran totally ignored me.

While my aunt and three cousins discussed the situation, Bran appeared unable to comprehend the idea, and seemed genuinely shocked, "He was not only able to get inside, but he walked around for a while?"

Gwen looked straight at Bran with a bit of a smirk. "Well, Julian Drake didn't have the same luck his cousin did. I'm fairly certain he burned his knuckles knocking on the glass front door to the store."

Bran snorted in reply. Ivy giggled and Holly looked serious. Which made me recall Gwen's comment about being surprised that Julian was even able to get that close to the shop's doorway. My stomach tied into knots.

What the hell was going on?

I fought the urge to raise my hand as I asked, "Is Duncan Quinn being able to get inside of Enchantments, significant somehow?"

Again they ignored me. Bran and Aunt Gwen seemed only to be talking to each other and the twins now.

"After he left the shop, an herbal ward fell. It practically exploded when it hit the floor," Ivy said to Bran, as the girls joined their little pow-wow, effectively shutting me out.

Hearing Ivy's comment about the exploding ward, Bran swore quietly. "Oh shit." And he seemed to notice the new floral arrangements on the work table for the first time.

"Oh shit, pretty much covers it," Ivy agreed a little too cheerfully.

"Hey!" I tried to get a word in.

"So, you're creating newer, stronger wards for all the thresholds," Bran said, right over me.

Aunt Gwen gestured to the work table and the brand new herbal arrangements. "For both the shop and the house."

"Hello, I am standing right here."

"Have you contacted the coven?" Bran asked his mother. Again, totally disregarding the rest of us lesser beings. Those lesser beings being myself.

Aunt Gwen nodded to him. "I did. They are all taking precautions."

"That's good." Holly's curls bounced as she nodded her head in agreement.

"Hey!" I shouted. "Maybe you've all forgotten that there is another damn person in the room. Someone you've kept secrets from, and who has no idea what the in the hell is going on!"

"Autumn," Holly pleaded, "Don't be angry. Not now."

"You are too much of a magickal novice to understand how serious this is." Bran said to me in a condescending tone.

"Fuck you, Bran." I was so tired, from the drama filled day, and angry, that I didn't even stop to think that I had never dropped the 'F bomb' in front of my aunt before. Until now.

"Watch your language!" Aunt Gwen snapped.

And then Bran and I were shouting insults back and forth at each other.

"Stay away from Duncan Quinn and his family!" Bran ordered.

"Mind your own damn business!" I shouted back. Merlin ran across my feet and went to sit by Holly.

"Bran, don't be such an ass!" Ivy yelled at her brother, as she was now standing at my side.

"Shut up Ivy!" Bran snarled at his sister.

Suddenly, a book sailed across the room all by itself, straight at Bran's head. My cousin ducked and the book bounced off the wall and fell to the floor.

"I won't miss next time!" Ivy yelled at her brother.

He straightened up and looked at his sister incredulously. His mouth worked. No sound came out.

As Ivy and I shouted at Bran, I had a second to realize that the flying book was just a warning. It made a weird kind of sense that heightened emotions would make for stronger, wilder magick.

The lights started to flicker and pop. A couple more books fell off the bookshelf, a sure sign that Ivy was rapidly losing control. Bran and I continued to argue at top volume with each other, while Ivy took my side. Merlin began to howl from the couch, and Holly, pale and shaking beside him, pleaded with everyone to stop fighting. Considering she could feel everyone's angry emotions, her distress must have been terrible.

Then with a loud boom that — I swear to god — sounded like a clap of thunder, my aunt raised her hands and simultaneously pushed out her magick. "Enough!" She shouted.

It was like getting hit with a big pillow right in the face. The force of her magick didn't hurt. It only startled me and shut me up, which I suppose was the point. All of us fell silent.

Bran took a breath to say something, and Gwen whipped her head around and told him, "You are all bickering like children! One more word, out of any of you, and I swear I'll strike all of you mute."

Ivy started to speak and it came out as a croaky sounding cough. *Whoa,* Aunt Gwen was not kidding. I had never seen her like this. I reached back for Ivy's hand and gave it a warning squeeze. Wisely, she stopped struggling to speak.

As I watched, Aunt Gwen reined in her temper. "All of you need to sit down, and calm down." She said in a softer, scarier tone of voice, "Right now."

Bran went and reluctantly sat on the window seat, but I remained standing, as did Ivy. It wasn't easy to stay still, feeling the weight and pressure of her magick. It cost me a bit, but I refused to back down. So, I learned right then and there that it is *not* comfortable going up against another Witch's will. Especially when they were pissed off and frustrated, like Aunt Gwen was now.

However, I stubbornly stayed where I was. Hand in hand, Ivy and I stood there. Both of us uncomfortable, but defiant.

"Autumn, you are so like your father," She said in a frustrated tone of voice. "He was strong *and* stubborn too." Then she sighed and I felt her magick ease up a bit.

"He and I used to have some pretty spectacular fights when we were kids. He had the same gift Ivy does. Seeing you use magick to shoot that book at Bran reminded me." Gwen laughed to Ivy.

"Really?" Ivy beamed at her mother, and then grinned at me, apparently thrilled with the thought that she shared something with her uncle.

"Oh yes. I wasn't as quick as Bran, he got me more than a few times."

Okay, color me confused. "Dad had telekinesis?" I had simply presumed he was like me, a Seer. And obviously I was way off on that assumption. "I never saw him use any magick." I told her.

"He was better with herbal spells." Gwen admitted. "But if you really ticked him off, then things would start to fly. Literally."

"Landscaping. That makes sense. He could still work with the plants. But telekinesis? I had no idea." I said. *Had I even know the man at all?*

"I'm not surprised. When you were a toddler, he abjured his gifts." Aunt Gwen laid a comforting hand on my shoulder.

"Why?" Holly, Ivy, and I all asked at the same time.

"Your mother told him he could either stay here and continue to practice alone, or he could leave behind his legacy and live a normal life with her and you."

"So, she gave him an ultimatum." I frowned.

"She did. The magickal world frightened her." Aunt Gwen said with a sad smile to Bran.

I tried to wrap my mind around that. My father had, what was the word Aunt Gwen used? *Abjured* his powers? So he gave up his magick for my mother. I couldn't help but imagine how horrified she must have been when her daughter ended up inheriting the Bishop family legacy of magick. I suppose that explained why she had staunchly ignored all of the manifestations of my abilities as I grew up. My dreams that came true, my very accurate intuition and hunches... She probably did not want to deal with the reality of it.

"I wonder if he ever regretted it." I sighed. It seemed like such a waste to me.

"He never regretted his life with you, Autumn. That much I am absolutely sure of," my aunt said confidently.

Meanwhile, Bran looked like he was on a slow boil, over on the window seat. Face red with temper, he grabbed the book that Ivy had 'sent' air mail across the room and shook it at her. "Damn it Ivy, you used magick against me!"

Ivy raised one eyebrow and sneered. "Bran, if I would've really meant to hit you with that, I would have." She waited a beat and then added, "Sorry." Which sounded less than sincere.

Bran just sputtered.

Aunt Gwen took advantage of the lull in the argument. "Bran, apologize to Autumn."

The house phone rang and Aunt Gwen cocked her head to the side. "I have to get that." Apparently she had a witchy/ telepathic version of caller ID, without her having to see the phone readout. "Behave yourselves for a few moments," she warned us. Then Aunt Gwen went quickly out of the turret room and over into her adjoining bedroom to pick up the extension. In a moment we all heard her quietly speaking to the caller.

We stared at each other for a few seconds. I suppose we were all acting like a bunch of little kids, which was pretty bad when you consider that Bran was twenty nine, I was about to turn twenty-four, and the twins were seventeen.

Bran rolled his eyes. "I'm sorry you're a novice," he said as he raked an aggravated hand through his short red hair.

"Yeah? Well, I'm sorry you're such a condescending ass," I said softly and with feeling.

Bran stood and walked up to me. He bent down, and leaned into my face a little bit. He stared intently into my eyes and seemed to be looking for something. After a couple of seconds he stepped back a bit and gave me a different, almost considering look. I didn't move a muscle during his little power play.

Finally, he let out a sigh and then rudely shouldered me out of the way, as he stalked over to replace the flying book. With the book shoved back into place he turned to me and said, "Consider that in this subject we *do* know more than you do. So, listen to my mother and stay away from the Drake family."

"You are not the boss of me." I said with my hands on my hips.

Was that a mature comeback or what? Even Holly laughed.

Bran crossed his arms over his chest. His expression was as serious as I have ever seen it. "Autumn, I have been around the Drake family all of my life. Bad things happen to anybody who gets in their way."

"Before we get off track, again," Holly interjected. "Autumn needs access to those family journals."

I agreed. "Yeah, this whole family feud thing is ridiculous. I'm not going to only take your word for it, or listen to town gossip." I frowned at him and then asked, "Plus, you didn't answer me before. Didn't you work with Duncan Quinn?"

Bran rubbed his forehead like he had a headache brewing, "Yes, I have worked with Quinn, in my capacity as the head of the historical archives at the University library. It's my job, to assist people who come to do research and to help them locate the documents."

"So you've met him. And didn't bother getting to know him? You just made snap judgment based on gossip and old grudges?" I accused him.

"I don't have to 'get to know him'." Bran's voice rose as he used air quotes, and then he caught himself and tried to continue more calmly. "He's a part of the Drake family. From when our ancestors first dealt with that family until today, they have all been nothing but evil." Bran said

"I didn't realize you were such a bigot. It's an ugly look for you Bran." I said to my cousin and I watched his face darken in temper.

"You are going to want to watch that sarcasm with me, *cousin*." He practically snarled the last word.

"Sarcasm is my super power." I flipped my long hair back over my shoulders, and crossed my arms over my chest.

A light bulb in the lamp on the table next to Holly blew out with a muffled pop, and the overhead lights started flickering again. I peered up at the light fixture and stepped out from under it. Was that Bran causing the lights to go wonky? Or was it all of the angry energy the family had put out? That was bound to do something to the electricity.

Aunt Gwen had finished her phone call and had returned to the room. She stood next to Holly and listened to Bran and I argue.

"Their family history speaks for itself," Bran said.

"Obsess much?" I said to Bran. "This supposed history you are so wrapped up in, those journals and old spell books, the old wives tales, have nothing to do with me."

I confronted my aunt. "You can hardly expect me to believe your story about this other family and our history without any proof. Expecting me to fall in line because of an old story handed down through the generations is unrealistic, and it's unfair."

Aunt Gwen looked thoughtful after my little speech.

"If Autumn is supposed to share in the legacy of magick, then she needs to know *everything*." Holly said. "Who our enemies are... and why. She needs to know all of our family history. Not only the parts you think she might be ready to handle." Holly rubbed her chin over the top of Merlin's kitty head. Now that the more volatile emotions were easing up, she seemed more comfortable.

I tried for a little of that calm myself. I dropped the defensive crossed arm pose and took a deep breath. When I spoke to my aunt, I was about as calm as I was liable to get. "I may have a lot to learn about the family legacy and magick. But I *will* learn. I just found out that my father stopped practicing his Craft because of my mother, and I don't understand the choice he made. But if those Bishop family journals also belonged to him, then they now belong to me. I'd like to see those journals. Now." I said to my aunt quietly.

Bran, naturally, and immediately, balked at my request.

At the rate we were going, with Bran arguing that I was too inexperienced to be reading the old spell-books, Holly quietly insisting that I should see them, Ivy loudly and ironically asking if anyone else was sick of the drama fest, and Gwen trying to keep us from blowing up the house... I was never going to see these 'all important' journals.

The lights continued to flicker, which made me

wonder how often these folks had to replace light bulbs in all the lamps. And you know what? I was so done talking. It was time for some action.

But where would the books be? I wondered. While Gwen tried to keep everyone calm, I considered my options, and decided to try something new. I'd attempt to gather psychic information from a specific person, on purpose. I was sort of on a roll with the abilities today, why not try it now?

Now, from a psychic standpoint, peeking into someone else's head, without an invitation, is pretty rude. But, I have to admit, it really pissed me off that my father had kept so many secrets both about my abilities, and his family from me. Also, I rationalized; I was living in a house full of practicing Witches. Maybe it was past time to stretch my wings a bit and see what I could do.

I looked at them all and considered. If Holly could sense an injury through touch, what would I be able to do if I deliberately touched someone with the intention of gaining information while using The Sight?

Since Bran was annoying me the most at the moment, I chose him as my target. Truth be told, I had no remorse about strolling through his head uninvited. I let all of the arguing flow past me and, since no one was looking at me anyway, I closed my eyes for a moment and concentrated on Bran. He stood there, within arms reach and still arguing with his sisters.

Find the family bond, I thought to myself. *We share*

grandparents after all, our parents were siblings. I concentrated harder and told myself, *find that blood connection.* Then I stretched out with my psychic abilities. Even though it pained me to do so, I focused on the family bond, the link between Bran and me.

I felt Bran's personal energy easily enough. I imagined that it would be angry and flickering out from him in a shade of red. Everyone has some sort or energetic shield — an aura — around them, even non-magickal folks. Witches, I had recently learned, tend to have well defined auras and they typically turn them into strong energetic shields. But I had an advantage. Bran had no idea of what I was plotting, and I moved fast. From a magickal point of view, he never even saw me coming.

I opened my eyes and started to reach out my hand, I envisioned my own aura to be a bright vibrant purple. I had read somewhere that purple was a power color for psychics, so that's what I chose. I took a deep breath, like I was about to jump off a diving board, and with intention, firmly grabbed a hold of Bran's wrist. Between the physical contact, both of us being angry, and the unfortunate blood bond, this made for a strong psychic link. His personal energy did not even slow me down.

I heard him yelp in surprise at my clamping down on his arm, and then I stopped hearing anything at all. Everyone in the room faded away, and I was no longer standing in the turret room in the middle of a family argument. I was instead strolling through Bran's head and looking into a memory of my cousin's.

Seeing his actions through his memories, I watched Bran go into a spacious walk in closet that was off to one side of his room. The closet was huge and all arranged with a fancy closet organizer kit. He reached up and pulled down on one of a dozen ornate brass hooks, mounted high inside the closet, where belts and ties were hung. With a click, a hidden door popped open on the wall beneath the brass hooks. Then Bran reached in and pulled out an old leather bound book. The memory started to fade, became fuzzy and then slid away.

I let my breath out in a rush and released Bran's wrist. The room spun slightly, but I held my ground and went for a sneer in my cousin's general direction.

"Hey!" He said, rubbing his wrist. "I didn't know you could do that! And damn it, I sure as hell did not give you permission!"

"Autumn, what did you do?" Gwen asked me in a chiding tone.

"She scanned my memories." Bran said outraged.

"She did?" Ivy laughed at her brother, and slung an arm around my shoulder. "Ooh, let's add postcognition to the girl's talents!"

"She's had virtually no training." Bran said as he glared at me, "I *felt* her sift through my memories! She shouldn't be able to do that."

I tried to cover up how nauseous and light headed I

felt with sarcasm. So I put my hands on my hips and raised an eyebrow at him, "Well Bran, maybe you're not that talented of a Witch, because it sure was *easy.*"

"Oh really?" He narrowed his eyes, smiled challengingly, and stepped a few paces back. He clapped the palms of his hands together sharply. As I watched, he pulled them apart and a golden ball of light appeared between his hands.

Ivy let go of me in a hurry and scampered back a few feet.

Dumbfounded, I stood there while the ball of light started to crackle and glow brighter. I glanced from the ball of light held between his hands and then up to his face. His eyes were practically glowing a neon green and his expression was tough as nails. Honestly, he scared the crap out of me. *Bran?* I thought to myself, *Bran the uptight, conservative 'librarian' was capable of this?*

CHAPTER 7

"Bran," Gwen laid her hand calmly on her son's arm, "Stop, you're frightening her."

Maybe the calm, matter-of-fact tone of Gwen's voice did the trick. As I stood there with my heart pounding and watched, Bran's expression changed. He closed his eyes and seemed to concentrate. He took a deep breath in, and slowly brought his hands back together. Then, Bran opened them and pushed his hands down towards the floor. The ball of crackling light fizzled out and faded away with a small pop. Bran blew his breath out slowly, opened his eyes, and regarded me steadily. It didn't help much that his eyes still seemed to be glowing.

I heard a roaring sound in my ears, I felt my face get very hot, and then my knees went bye-bye. The next thing I knew my butt hit the floor. I saw spots in front of my eyes and felt someone shove my head between my knees. "Holy shit." I heard myself say in a breathless voice.

After a bit, I realized that someone was stroking my hair and speaking in a gentle tone of voice. They smelled like sunscreen and red gold curls wavered in and out of focus in front of my eyes. I knew that hair and that voice... Holly. It was Holly. And after everything I had seen today, I suppose it made sense that the empathic cousin would be the one to offer comfort.

She pressed a hand to my shoulder and I felt her fingers grow warm. What ever magick she was doing started to work right away, my head stopped spinning, my stomach stopped churning, and the roaring sounds in my ears faded away. I raised my head and looked in her eyes. The pale blue-green color seemed to be more intense, but there she was, crouching down next to me like a catcher behind home plate, calm, pretty, and serene as ever.

"Better?" Holly asked me.

"Yeah." I blinked a couple of times. I did feel better. I looked away from her eyes and tried to focus on my surroundings.

"Stand up now." Holly directed me. While her voice was soft, it was also firm. I climbed slowly to my feet, with her help.

"Well, that was… *different*." I announced.

"Okay, I'm going to ask," Ivy stepped up and grinned at me, "What did you pull out of Bran's head?"

"He has a hidden compartment in his closet." I said. "Pulling down on one of the brass hooks opens the panel."

Aunt Gwen merely raised an eyebrow at my announcement, and probably at my aggressive psychic maneuver, but she nodded her head in confirmation.

"Good job, cousin!" Ivy gave a knuckle bump. "Let's go check it out." She motioned to Holly who nodded her agreement. Merlin scampered out into the hallway, and then stopped as if waiting for us.

As soon as we stepped out into the hall, the door to the room closed smartly behind us. Ivy was showing off a bit, but it might slow Bran down. Maybe. My head was still spinning after seeing what *he* could do. Holly and Ivy grinned at each other as the three of us walked down the winding hall and headed towards what the girls called the Fortress of Solitude — AKA: Bran's bedroom suite.

Merlin pranced along with us, and Holly actually smiled at hearing the turret room door rattle as Bran tried to open it. His outrage about the three of us going, uninvited, into his room, was easy to hear.

"Oh my, he's really pissed off. How tragic." Holly said surprisingly straight faced. Which made me chuckle.

Then Holly looked at me seriously, "He shouldn't have raised energy like that in front of you, not when you've never seen anybody do something like that before. You're a Seer, of course you would be able to see the manifestation of that much magickal energy."

I stopped dead. "Hold up a second," I said. "So what

are you saying? Not everyone would be able to see that energy ball thing?"

"No, actually, a mundane, non-magickal person would see nothing. An empath would feel it. But a Seer would see the physical manifestation very clearly." Holly explained.

"So what did you two see?" I asked them.

Ivy gave me an arched look, "I sensed the energy build and heard the crackle right as he clapped he hands together."

"Which is why you got the hell out of the way," I surmised.

"My mama didn't raise no fool." Ivy said with a thick southern accent.

I laughed.

"I could *feel* his anger," Holly explained next, as she pressed a fist to her stomach, "The anger raised the energy ball very quickly, so it manifested more dramatically, but I don't have to see it with my own eyes to know it's there."

I took that in and considered. I was going to have to start taking notes to keep track of all of this if I really wanted to learn.

Holly opened the door to her brother's room and announced, "Besides, scaring you like that was a dick move."

My eyes popped wide and I started to laugh. Clearly I needed to look a little deeper at the twins, instead of simply thinking — Holly: sweet, compassionate, and kind. Ivy: dramatic, gothic, and funny.

Holly looked at me seriously, "I'm not all sweetness and light, you know."

I reached out and playfully tagged on one of those wild, strawberry blonde curls. "Well thanks for the rescue in there. Oh, and Holly…I like you better when you're sassy."

That comment made her light up. She gave me a friendly hip bump and said, "I really want to see those family journals again, for myself."

Ivy wiggled her eyebrows at the two of us, "Well then, let's get to it."

I hesitated right outside of the doorway to Bran's room, half expecting some type of magickal whammy to hit me as I crossed into the room. I took a breath, prepared myself, and stepped in.

Inside his fancy, designer looking bedroom, the walls were painted a warm ivory. The room boasted dark, heavy, obviously antique furniture and a huge neatly made bed, with a hunter green bedspread. I saw a leather sofa and a few small tables set up to create a small reading area as well. I felt a slight buzz in the air but other than that, nothing. Ivy and Holly stepped in easily behind me and Merlin padded in, sniffing the air expectantly. We all stood still, waiting. I felt the buzz fade. And then... *nothing* happened.

No whammy.

No energetic smack down.

No magickal repercussions from entering his

bedroom at all. And wasn't that interesting?

Feeling bolder by the moment I marched right into his huge closet with my cousins following me, leaving Merlin to explore Bran's previously 'off-limits' bedroom. I reached up towards the brass hooks, as I had seen Bran do in his own memory, chose the one I thought was correct, and pulled it down.

With a solid click, a medium sized panel swung open. Holly and Ivy both smiled, and together the three of us reached out and swung the small doorway fully open. There, on recessed wooden bookshelves about three feet wide and four feet tall, in shades of faded blue, green, brown and black, the old journals and hand written spell books, called grimoires, were arranged. Some of the books were leather covered journals and some were hard back books.

Oh wow. Seeing all those antique books gave my inner museum nerd a thrill. "Do you have a suggestion on which book I should start with?" I asked and wondered how the family told the books apart.

"Let me try using psychometry." she said. I started to step back but Holly snagged my left hand. She explained that holding my receptive hand while she scanned the books would help her be able to divine which book would be the best for me to start with.

"I'm not sure what psychometry is," I admitted.

"Psychometry, or clairtangency, is the psychic ability to gather information by touch." Holly said. "For example, I can read objects by touching them with my fingertips, or by holding small objects in the palm of my hand."

Ivy wiggled up beside us. "Yeah. Like, if she found a set of keys picked them up and then concentrated, she would *feel* who the keys belonged to or maybe get emotional impressions about the owner. Stuff like that."

So Holly held my hand, and using her own right, dominant hand she ran her fingers lightly above the spines of the old spell books and journals on the shelves. Her eyes were closed and her head was tilted slightly to the side she scanned them.

"This one has the strongest vibrations." Holly pulled an old leather bound journal gently from the shelf.

Aunt Gwen cleared her throat, and we all turned. "That journal is an excellent place to start." She stood there, outside of the closet door and waited.

"Didn't figure that locked door would hold against your magick very long." Ivy grinned at her mother.

Aunt Gwen playfully smacked Ivy upside the head as she walked past. "Brat." She said, which made Ivy grin. Then she held out her hand for the volume. When Holly handed it to her, Aunt Gwen gently opened the cover and scanned the first page. "Yes, this one was written by Eliza. She was a sister to Patience." She held the book out to me. "These books are irreplaceable, and must stay inside of the house at all times," she warned me.

"Do you have any protective cotton gloves to keep the pages from being damaged?" I asked her. "These books should be handled very carefully. Please tell me that you have some archival boxes for storage, and that you know to keep the pages out of direct sunlight to lessen the chance of the ink fading?"

"Yes, we know how to care for the old grimoires." Bran announced from the doorway, as he scowled at us all.

Then, I kid you not; he marched past me, reached into a drawer from his fancy closet organizer, and produced a couple packages of white gloves. He handed them to me.

I was relieved that he took the whole magickal librarian-historian thing seriously. Early American history was precious. If it wasn't for the personal magickal information the family said the books held, I'd have argued that those journals belonged in a museum.

Bran took a deep breath and looked down at his feet. "I apologize if I frightened you or made you feel unwelcome in my home... our home." He quickly corrected himself.

Three guesses as to who had made him come and apologize.

"Why did you?" I asked him flat out.

"I'm not ready to talk about it, yet." He admitted. He looked at his mother. "I'll work on it, okay?"

"Okay." I answered with suspicion, and wasn't sure if he was addressing his mother or me.

"But don't barge into my room whenever you feel

like it," Bran said. Then he added with a frown as he saw Merlin sitting in the closet doorway, "And keep that rotten cat out of here, too." He added to his sisters.

He's just a prince, isn't he? I thought to myself. Maybe if I rapped his head against the wall... maybe that would have some effect on his attitude. "I'll knock before entering." I conceded.

Bran looked unimpressed.

"Tell you what, how about if I let Gwen know if I am taking a journal out of the super-secret hidey hole?" I suggested.

"I guess that will be okay. But hands off my suits!" Bran snagged Ivy by the back of her shirt and tugged her away from the line of neatly hung clothes. Then he backed towards the racks of all of his various items of conservative clothing, his arms protectively wide as if to block us.

As if I'd be interested in his—wait a minute. Was that a motorcycle jacket hanging in the corner? A fabulous, vintage, leather motorcycle jacket? What in the world was that doing in a closet full of conservativeness?

Bran noticed my eyeballing the jacket "And if you even think about touching my leather jackets, I'll take you out personal."

Gwen frowned at her son. "Bran, that's not quite what I meant when I told you to be more loving and welcoming to Autumn. We are a family."

"Yeah well, family love and all that..." Bran said.

"But touch my leather jackets and die." His eyes narrowed as she looked at his sisters and me.

Gwen leveled a look at her son, and Bran hunched his shoulders a bit in reaction to his mother's expression.

"Sorry," he cleared his throat and then said. "Now will you all please get out of my closet?"

We all began to file out, Gwen holding the journal, and me with the packages of gloves. Holly followed her. Ivy, of course, had to go back and run her hands over Bran's display of designer ties and make yummy sounds behind her mother's back. I reached in, grabbed Ivy by her arm, and hauled her out before Bran could retaliate.

Bran followed us out and shut the closet door behind him. I looked curiously around at Bran's room. I noted a big desk and fancy computer, and what else? More shelves for books. "I don't think I have been in your room more than once, unless it was to hand you your laundry." I commented.

"Yeah? Well let's not get too cozy in here. I like my privacy."

"Jeez, you really are a jerk."

"Bet your ass." He shot back.

I had to laugh at that. Aunt Gwen, Holly and Ivy were deep in discussion over the old journal, and I walked over to check out the top of Bran's dresser. My cousin had it set up like an altar. I looked, but did not touch the magickal tools.

Besides I had already taken an uninvited stroll through Bran's head today... I didn't want to be too pushy. On the top of the dresser were a couple of taper candles in ornate, old fashioned, silver candlesticks, and a wand made out of copper and topped with an amethyst point. There was an incense burner shaped like a mini cauldron and a wooden disc with a pentacle, the upright five-pointed star, burnt into it. All around the edge of the pentacle, ivy and holly leaves were added to the design. I had seen similar, simpler wooden pentacles for sale in the shop, but this seemed unique.

"Is this custom made?" I asked Bran. "I haven't seen this design at the shop before."

"It is," he agreed. "It was a gift for my birthday, from a friend." Bran took a breath and looked over at his mother and sisters who were deep in discussion. "Look," he said softly, trying to keep our conversation private. "I really don't want to make you angry and I don't know Duncan Quinn very well. He might be as nice as you say, but do yourself a favor. Be careful. And stay away from his family."

"I met his cousin, Julian. He seemed like a snob." I agreed.

"He's worse than that. A friend of mine dated Julian a few years ago... Women tend to find him attractive, but he has a bad reputation."

"How do you mean?" I asked.

Bran took a hold of my elbow and steered me even farther away from his sisters. "What do you think I mean? My friend told me that she had to fight him off when he didn't want to take 'no' as an answer."

I cringed a little. "Oh god. Was she okay?"

"Yes, but she ended up having to walk a couple of miles alone, in the dark, to get home that night. When she got there, she found her purse tossed at the bottom of the driveway and cell phone smashed."

"Thanks for the warning," I said.

Bran asked me how I had met Duncan this morning and, as we sat on the leather sofa, I briefly told Bran about running into Duncan, and how he had walked me home. Bran also asked me to tell him what I had noticed when Duncan came into our store, so I filled him in on that too. I did *not* however tell Bran about the comment Duncan Quinn had made on magick and families while we were up at the pool.

Did you think yours was the only family in town with a legacy of magick? That sounded vaguely threatening now and I needed to think carefully about what he had said.

I think Bran and I realized we were actually sitting together and talking, almost pleasantly, at about the same time, as an awkward silence suddenly fell between us. I stood up and made an excuse about needing to go take a shower after swimming.

Merlin took that moment to strut across Bran's bedroom floor with a silk necktie dangling from his mouth like a trophy. I saw him out of the corner of my eye and choked back a laugh.

Determined to let Bran know he was not intimidated, Merlin slinked up to next him and sat, just waiting for Bran to react to him and his 'prize'. He did not notice the cat's presence at first. Then Merlin deliberately leaned into him. Bran looked down, feeling the brush of the cat against his leg, and then swore.

Like a sailor on shore leave. Wow. Who knew he even had that kind of vocabulary?

Bran dove after the cat swearing about him ruining his expensive tie. Merlin streaked out of the room fully expecting, and apparently delighted, that Bran was going to chase him.

It sounded like a war with Bran pounding down the stairs and shouting after the cat. Holly shoved the journal at Ivy and then raced after them trying to help. Ivy dropped down on Bran's bed and laughed. I heard the unmistakable sound of a lamp getting knocked over and I had a flash of the little celestial blue lamp on the table on the second floor landing. I cringed and looked down the hallway to confirm my suspicions.

"The little blue lamp is down," I said. "I don't think he broke it, though."

"We will talk later about ethical behavior, you and I," Gwen told me seriously.

Yeah, I supposed my maneuver of looking uninvited through Bran's memories was going to earn me a lecture. That's okay; I had a few things I wanted to know more about anyway. Like energy balls, what other sorts of talents my father possessed, and whether or not

I had inherited any of them

Then as the sounds of running and yelling increased in volume, Aunt Gwen rolled her eyes to the ceiling and gave up. "I think we can safely say this family meeting is adjourned."

***

Over the next few days I read through Eliza's journal. It was interesting from a historical point of view and there were little spells and charms that I supposed were important in Colonial life, but not too useful today. A charm for making sure the cows gave plenty of milk, a spell that ensured a bountiful vegetable garden, a few herbal remedies for reducing fevers and treating gout, whatever the hell gout was.

Eliza mentioned briefly in her journal her concerns for her sister, Patience, and that she was concerned about James Drake's 'dalliance' with her sister. I actually went and looked up that word making sure I understood the meaning. To my amusement, I discovered it was what folks would call a fling, or a hook up, today. But most of Eliza's focus had been on her marriage to a farmer named Zeke, her children, her Craft, and their daily lives. But so far the journal had told me very little about the supposed magickal feud.

I had my first classes at the University, and my new schedule gave me Tuesdays and Thursdays off. That allowed me plenty of time to work on my museum education and museum studies intro classes. As well as a chance to study up on the legacy of magick that I was becoming a part of. Spell books were off limits to me for the time being, Gwen had told me. However, I could review books on the basics or theory of magick.

Aunt Gwen did indeed have a talk with me about using psychic abilities on your own family members the morning after the show down in the turret. I also got another speech on the dangers of using psychic abilities and magick in an intrusive or manipulative way. I shut my mouth and figured finding out that information had been worth the cost of a lecture.

In turn I asked her for more information about the wards at the shop and the house, and inquired why they were even necessary in the first place. Apparently, it was like a psychic and magickal alarm system. If something tried to cross the wards or breech the defenses, the wards would give the occupants, or the Witch of the house, a bit of a psychic nudge in warning. Wards were used for deflecting negativity, making it harder for an intruder to physically break in; they also banished evil and kept out other magickal beasties.

As to my aunt's warning to stay away from Duncan Quinn, I decided to wait and see for myself about Duncan and his family.

On Friday, I juggled a stack of heavy books, my purse, and my laptop while on my way to class. A kicky breeze blew my long hair all to hell and back. I blew at the strands in my face and kept moving. I had exactly fifteen minutes to get to my Museum Education class, which was being held at a local history museum. I was excited and raring to go, not only at the idea of having my class inside of the museum, but at the opportunity to learn more about the history of the area.

I went straight to the information desk and asked for directions to the museum's board room. I felt a little thrill when I was issued a security card and a museum ID badge. The receptionist informed me that I would have to sign in and out and passed me a clip board. I clipped my ID to the neck of my royal blue shirt, smoothed my hair back, scooped up my books again, and headed quickly for the board room.

I went around the corner and smacked solidly into someone. "Oof!" I managed to save my laptop, after a hell of a juggle, but the books hit the floor and made a horrible racket. I had a split second to silently curse my own klutziness and another to identify the person I'd smacked into as male.

"I apologize. Are you alright?" The man said.

"Sorry." I raised my eyes to discover Julian Drake, and my stomach flipped in response. Julian was indeed the classic tall, dark, and handsome type, but it wasn't physical attraction that had my stomach doing backflips, it was anxiety. I took an automatic step back, recalling what Bran had told me about him.

"Well, hello again." He smiled at me, and gallantly bent down and gathered up my books. "Here you go." He held them out.

"Thank you." I said politely and attempted to stack them on top of my laptop case. The books began to slide immediately.

"On second thought..." He reached over and neatly took the books back. "Let me help you."

"That's okay." I tried to politely decline.

"You're headed to the board room, right?" Julian asked.

"Yes, I am." I studied him. He stood there acting perfectly courteous, in a fancy dark suit, and somehow I felt a little embarrassed for feeling nervous of him.

He made an 'after you' gesture and I decided to let him carry the books and get it over with. I hustled to the board room and saw about a dozen other people gathering around a large conference table. I went straight to the first open chair and set my laptop and purse down.

Julian set the books on the table for me. "The Education Director of the museum teaches this class doesn't she?"

I wondered how he'd known that.

"She's a friend of mine. Let me introduce you."

"Oh that's okay, you don't have to." I said as Julian put his hand at the small of my back and I found myself guided along to meet the director.

Julian made the introductions smoothly, and I was uncomfortably aware that his hand stayed against my back the entire time. In contrast to his behavior in the flower shop, Julian was suave and acted the perfect gentleman, which made me wonder what he was up to. Introductions complete, I went straight back to the conference table and sat down. His hand at my back had made me twitchy, and not in a good way. I let out a quiet sigh of relief until I saw him coming my way again.

"Autumn." Julian laid a gentle hand on my shoulder.

I tried for a calm neutral expression as I looked back at him from over my shoulder. "Thanks for your help." I said quietly. Hoping he would take the hint and leave.

"My pleasure." His lips curved up a little, and with a casual wave he let himself out of the board room.

"Wow." A young blonde woman next to me whistled out a quiet breath. "Is that your boyfriend?" She swiveled in her chair and watched Julian walk away.

'No. He's an... acquaintance." I finally decided to call him.

"He's seriously gorgeous." She said under her breath, and then focused on me. "Hi, I'm Emily."

"Nice to meet you." I said automatically, and then shifted my attention to the director who began to speak to the class.

Three hours later I headed back outside with Emily. We were chatting about the class and it was fully dark. We parted ways and I carted all of my things to my truck. I slid my laptop and books across the bench seat. My mind on the class and the massive reading list that had been assigned, I was fishing around for my keys when I first noticed the smell.

I looked up at the dashboard to discover a rose. I flinched, and started looking around the parking lot, wondering who had left the flower. "That'll teach me to leave my door unlocked." I said to myself.

I started up my truck and locked the doors. Then I gently picked up the thorny stem. I had a hunch that the flower was pilfered from a nearby garden. The red and white rose was half open and very fragrant. There was a little card lying under the flower. It read.

Enjoy your classes. If I can be of any help, please let
me know.
Julian

I flipped over the back of the card and discovered it was his business card for the museum. And Julian Drake was on the board of directors. Which meant the chances of seeing him again at the museum would be high. I noted that his personal cell phone was also listed on the card.

Not sure how I felt about that, I tucked the card in one of my books. It wouldn't be a smart move ticking off a guy on the board of the museum where I would be working, studying, and doing my internship. I set the rose next to me, and decided it wasn't the flower's fault that the guy who sent it was mildly creepy. Besides, I supposed, I'd have to wait and see what, if anything, happened next.

***

We were rolling towards mid-September, the humidity and the heat were incredible. I went running in the evenings of my days off when it was cooler outside, and I never saw Duncan Quinn. Not even when I casually happened to jog by his family's home. I didn't do that too often, though, as the big stone house gave me the creeps now. I blamed that on Aunt Gwen and Bran's warnings about the Drake family.

Still, I imagined he was busy somewhere in town flipping and rehabbing houses, as I was busy settling into my new schedule with the family and grad school.

At least that's what I told myself.

I did see Julian at the Museum, usually as I arrived for my evening classes. He was always impeccably groomed, and polite. Julian was respected at the museum and everyone seemed to like him. Especially Emily. For the most part, he kept his distance from the grad students, which relived me, and disappointed Emily.

Feeling happy at having finished another week of classes, I cranked the AC on high in my pickup truck and headed out to go pick up the twins from school, as their shared car was in the shop.

Holly was telling Ivy about the big drama on her varsity cheer squad. Apparently a Senior, named Kellie, had broken an ankle, and was sidelined until November, which meant they would be pulling from the JV squad to fill the position.

I listened with half an ear as I navigated through town. I pulled into our neighborhood and then up to a four way stop sign. That was when I saw an officer in a crisp blue uniform and policeman's hat standing on the sidewalk on the driver's side of the car. He looked at me intently and gestured for me to stop with that 'halt' hand motion all cops use. It really stood out as he was wearing white gloves. I stayed at the stop sign and wondered what was going on.

I looked to the left and the right, but there were no other cars coming. I looked back at the cop and he was gone. That was weird, and I felt my stomach turn over.

"What are you waiting for, Autumn?" Ivy asked me.

"I could've sworn I saw a cop on the corner." I said half to myself. I double checked, saw no traffic and eased through the intersection. While the twins chattered on about the big cheer squad drama, I continued on down the street past the Drake's massive, creepy stone house, and on to the next stop sign.

I stopped again and waited for the car across from me to take its turn. I looked to my right and left. All was clear, so I took my foot off the brake and began to go through the intersection. Suddenly, a huge black bird flew right into the front windshield. "Whoa!" I yelped and stomped down on the truck's brakes.

At the same time, a black SUV roared through the intersection from my left, its radio blaring. Time seemed to slow down as the other vehicle missed the front bumper of my truck by inches and zoomed on without stopping. The crow bounced off our windshield, cawed loudly, scattered a few feathers, and then flew off.

We sat there for a second or two, frozen, and my breathing sounded loud to my own ears. If that crow hadn't flown into the windshield, I would not have stopped. I would have taken a direct, driver's side hit from that fast moving SUV. Crap, that was close!

"Is everybody okay?" I asked.

"What the hell did you hit?" Ivy demanded.

"A big crow," I said as I turned on the hazard flashers and put the truck in park. I heard Holly make a concerned sound for the bird, and I climbed out and looked around, but the stop-sign running SUV, and the crow were nowhere to be seen.

As I looked more closely at the windshield, I saw a chalky outline from where the bird had bounced off, and a large black feather resting on the hood of my tan truck. I reached out to pick up the feather and only then noticed that my hand was shaking.

Nope. Not gonna think about how close of a call that was. Best to get everybody home. Preferably in one piece. A car pulled up behind us in the intersection, and a woman stuck her head out the window to ask if we were okay. I waved, said yes, and got back in the truck. I set the feather on the front seat next to me.

Using her cell phone, Ivy snapped a picture of the weird but perfect chalky outline of the bird on the windshield.

I drove the rest of the short trip home very cautiously, and the girls were silent passengers. When I pulled in the driveway, we all climbed out and stood there staring at each other for a second.

"Good thing that crow bounced off the windshield," Ivy said very quietly.

"Otherwise that SUV would have hit us." I glanced down at the feather in my hand.

Holly reached out and took the long black plume. "Mom says that the crow is a messenger from the spirit realm."

"I think I recall my father once telling me a story, when I was little, about how crows were the messengers of the old gods." I let out a long breath. "Damn, that was close."

"You should save that feather," Holly suggested, and in unspoken agreement we began walking to the front porch. Holly suddenly seemed a lot older and wiser that your average seventeen year old. Probably came from being raised as a Witch.

My feet hit the front steps when I remembered that I had left my purse in the truck. Holly and Ivy headed inside, and I went back to go get my purse.

With it retrieved, I closed the cab door and saw someone standing near the end of the driveway, out on the sidewalk, beyond our wrought iron fence. It was the cop I had observed earlier, standing quietly and watching me.

He was close enough and I had plenty of time to get a good look at him. He had dark hair, buzzed short in a military looking cut. His shirt was starched and pressed, and his pants even had creases in them. His hat sat neatly on his head and I saw that he still had on white gloves. *Dress uniform...* the phrase floated in my mind. And where did that phrase come from?

My stomach jumped. What was he doing here? "Can I help you, officer?" I called politely over to him.

He looked down and smiled at the edge of the driveway, as if he was seeing something I could not.

Curious, I walked down closer to where he was standing. The longer I looked directly at him— the harder it was to focus on him, almost as if the edges of him shimmered. With all the discussion of wards in the past week I wondered if the property line was 'warded' as well. If it was enchanted against evil from entering— then it was protected against all sorts of things.

I laughed to myself as I mentally crossed vampires off the list. It was broad daylight, after all. As I stopped about six feet away from where he stood, I felt a noticeable drop in the temperature. Considering that it was in the high nineties today, the difference in the temperature made me shiver.

Vampire? No. But whatever I was seeing was not a regular person. My heart started to pound. "What do you want?" I asked him flatly. Then I noticed I was seeing my breath puff out on the air, as if it was cold outside.

The policeman's friendly brown eyes calmed me a bit. "Be safe," he said. With that, he tipped his hat to me, turned to walk back down the sidewalk, and vanished.

CHAPTER 8

And I do mean he vanished. As in, there one second and gone the next. I had actually seen someone go *poof*, right in front of my own eyes.

Goosebumps broke out on my arms and I shuddered, feeling the temperature swing back to hot and stuffy. *Congratulations Autumn*, I thought to myself. *You have seen and communicated with your first ghost.*

"Messenger from the spirit realm..." I recalled as I looked down at the feather I still clutched in my fist. Terrific. As if there hadn't been enough drama lately? I walked down to the end of the driveway and looked up and down the street to be sure.

Nope. No one was out walking, and everything was dead quiet.

Ha. Dead quiet. Shaking my head at my own inner monologue, I made myself turn around and walk calmly and deliberately back to the house.

It took everything I had not to look over my shoulder.

I made it to the big covered front porch without further incident. I let out a breath I hadn't even known I'd been holding. Feeling a little light-headed, probably from the adrenalin and from inadvertently holding my breath, I moved over to the front porch swing for a few moments. I sat on the wooden swing and watched the butterflies and hummingbirds zip through the front gardens and, well, I won't lie. I kept watch.

While I sat there waiting for my heart rate to slow down, I thought about what I had just seen, or *seen*. Call me old fashioned, but I had always figured ghosts typically appeared in a foggy graveyard or in a creepy old house during a dark, stormy night. It seemed spookier somehow, that this had happened to me in broad daylight. I knew next to nothing about ghosts. But I could fix that pretty quick, couldn't I?

Ten minutes later I had a haul of books from Gwen's room spread over my bed. They covered psychics, psychic abilities, ghost, and spirit communication. Boy I loved research, and these books appeared even more interesting than the one I was supposed to be reading, *An Introduction to Museum Studies*. Merlin peered up at me from the foot of the bed where I had disturbed his nap, then padded over and stretched out beside me. I took plenty of notes, and gave the psychic and paranormal books my undivided attention for a few hours.

It was well worth my time, and I soon discovered what the term *postcognitive* meant. When Ivy tossed that out after Bran's light show, I'd been too shell-shocked to ask.

So according to the reference books, it meant the experience of acquiring psychic information form the past. Depending on the ability of the individual; a postcognitive experience could manifest as hearing voices and music from the past, sensing old memories, or even having a clairvoyant vision of past events. Which is what I had done when I strolled through Bran's memories the other day. I took more notes on postcognition, and started to feel like I was getting a better idea on what I had been dealing with. I also decided to keep the ghostly police officer to myself, for now.

By six o'clock, my stomach was rumbling and I set the books aside, looking forward to the Chinese takeout that was being ordered tonight. I padded barefoot downstairs to find Holly and Ivy sitting at the kitchen table having a hushed discussion with Bran.

I stood out of sight, around the corner of the dining room, and shamelessly eavesdropped on the three of them. Seeing their heads close together, I could really see the family resemblance. Which, I admit, made me feel a little out of place again. Their voices were low, but I began to follow their discussion: what was to be done about the Drake family's current activities. Particularly, they did not seem happy about Julian being a new board member at the same museum where I was taking classes. I quietly backed up a few feet, and then purposefully walked back towards the kitchen humming to myself.

As I expected, the conversation switched off immediately, and I was met with three fairly strained smiles, which I pretended to be oblivious to.

"Hey guys, what's up?" I asked them, all smiles and pseudo good cheer.

Ivy and Holly jumped to their feet and began pulling dishes out of the cupboards to set the table. No, they didn't look guilty at all...

"We were discussing the ramifications of the Drakes' movement into our territory." Bran said.

I rolled my eyes, "Territory? You make this sound like a border skirmish."

"You are not far off. Duncan Quinn walked right into our store a few weeks ago." Bran reminded me.

"Yeah, and I take my classes at the museum where Julian is a board member every week."

"Yes we know." Bran narrowed his eyes. "I don't like that either."

"He seems well respected at the museum and he's been very polite every time I have seen him."

"Julian better leave you alone, or else." Bran growled.

"Or what?" I asked. "Spell books at twenty paces?"

Clearly frustrated with my snarkiness, he sighed long and loud.

"No wait, I'm getting a mental picture..." I put my hand to the bridge of my nose as if in deep concentration. "I foresee herbs and insults flying. A showdown at midnight…This town ain't big enough for the two of you, type of thing?"

"I accept that you are not ready to believe, or even understand the importance of, our history. However, the sarcasm is out of place and, quite frankly, offensive to this family." Bran lectured me while I stood there and grinned at him.

While Holly and Ivy stayed busy setting the table, Aunt Gwen had come in through the potting room. "Bickering again?" She asked as she set her purse down. Then she went straight to the fridge, pulled out a bottle of wine, poured herself a large glass, and proceeded to drink it. Straight down.

"Rough day?" I asked her, and smiled at her shooting back the wine.

"It was a long one." Gwen admitted.

I knew when to let an argument drop and pretend like all was fine and normal in the world. So I put that skill to use now. I offered to go pick up dinner, located my shoes and purse, and headed out to the truck.

A short while later, I was gathering up all of the bags of food from the Jade Dragon restaurant. My mind on the incredible smells coming from the bags, I moved towards the exit. Since my hands were full, I spun around and used my butt to push open the door. Suddenly the door was pulled open behind me.

I managed an "Oops!" as I over balanced and bobbled the bags of Chinese food.

A strong pair of calloused hands grabbed my shoulders steadying me, and a little electric shock, like a strong snap of static electricity, zipped right up my neck to the top of my head.

"Sorry!" A familiar laughing male voice said.

I looked over my shoulder and discovered none other than Duncan, standing there grinning down at me. Today, he was wearing a faded black t-shirt, dusty jeans, and well used work boots. He smelled pleasantly of saw dust and sweat. And there I was, practically in his arms. Again. "We *really* have to stop meeting like this." I muttered and straightened. Good grief, would I ever be around the man and not look like a klutz?

"Let me give you a hand." He chuckled and took a couple of the bags of food from me.

"That's alright." I started to protest, and he frowned at me. I realized he was only being friendly, and I had let all the family's talk get to me in the past few weeks. Determined to be friendly in return, I gestured to my truck, "I'm parked right over here."

Duncan turned and spoke to two other men that were with him, and they went inside the restaurant. As they were all dressed similarly; I guessed they must have come from their job site.

I opened the cab door, set the bags down on the bench seat, and then reached back for the bags Duncan held. Setting them in place, I saw Duncan frowning at the landscaping logo that was still on the door of the truck. I should probably have that removed, but I really hadn't worked up to it yet.

"Your father was a landscaper?" he asked.

"That's right."

"Do you know anything about landscaping?" He asked thoughtfully.

I raised an eyebrow at him, "Are you trying to offend me? I worked landscaping with my dad all through high school and every summer when I was in college. And then for another year and a half full time." I tilted my head and finished with, "Bet your ass I *know* landscaping."

"Really?" He said considering, "I could use someone with a good eye for landscape design at the house I'm flipping. The yard is trashed, and I want to have some low maintenance plants put in. Maybe add some flowers for color when the house goes on the market at the end of the month."

"Are you looking for advice or someone to plant the yard?" I asked him.

"Both." He said taking a pen and a business card out of his pocket. "Tell you what — why don't you come by this address tomorrow morning and I'll give you the tour. You can decide if you want to take the project on. If you want the job, then we can talk about your fee, afterwards." He wrote an address on the card and handed it to me.

Pleased, at both the opportunity to see him again and the chance of having a job opportunity fall into my lap, I accepted the card. We agreed that I would drop by around eight in the morning, and he left with a casual wave and headed inside to join his friends.

I tucked the card into my purse. What would the family think about this development? As I made the short drive back to the manor I decided to say nothing about bumping into Duncan again or his request. The family would flip if they thought I was considering working with a member of the Drake family.

I let myself in to the manor, my mind occupied on what I'd wear when I saw Duncan in the morning, and I tripped on the rug just inside the door. I caught myself and headed back towards the kitchen calling out that dinner had arrived.

Maybe I'll be graceful in my next life.

***

Saturday morning, I woke early as usual, and then waited impatiently until it was time to go meet Duncan. I took a critical look at my clothes, considered the high heat, and chose carefully. I had either seen the man while sweaty and disheveled from running, casual in shorts and a t shirt, wet and freaked out at the club pool, or wearing blue jean shorts and tripping into him at the Chinese restaurant. My mother would say it was vanity, but I figured it was more about making a good impression on a prospective client.

Realistically, I could not stroll over to the house in a dress and some cute strappy sandals. That was ridiculous, not to mention risky on a job site. However, I could at least make an effort to appear a bit more polished up than he had ever seen me before. I decided on a pretty amethyst colored tank top to go with my heavy khaki work shorts, compliments of my former nursery-employee days. I rooted through the colorful explosion of my sock drawer and then dug my old, sturdy shoes out of the closet. As I sat on the bench at the foot of the bed to put them on, I saw Merlin looking me over with a blink.

"What, too many colors together?" I asked him. My very own feline version of *What Not to Wear...* I had grabbed one yellow and purple striped sock and a solid royal blue one. They peeked cheerfully right above the edges of my shoes and made me grin.

No, my socks never matched, and I liked it that-a-way. A girl is allowed to have a few quirks after all, besides the whole "The Sight" thing at least.

Anyway, my Dad always told me when I was little that wearing socks that did not match would keep you from being faery led. You know, tricked by the little people. I smiled a bit as I looked at the framed picture of my father sitting on the mantle of the white painted brick fireplace in my new room. It was the last really good photo I had of him and me together.

To compensate for the sturdy shoes, I traded my glasses for contact lenses, painted on a neat, cat's eye stroke of black eyeliner, added a bit more eye shadow, and smeared on some tinted lip balm. For a change, I left my hair down, sprayed on a bit of lavender body spray, and called it good.

I snagged my purse and notebook and walked casually out into the hall, only to find Ivy waiting for me. "Where are you going?" she asked.

There was really no way to sneak out of this house, was there? "What are you doing up so early? You're going to blow your un-dead image, Ivy." I made a face, and tried to walk around her.

She shifted and blocked. "I had a dream about you. It woke me up, and I wondered where you were going so early."

Was that Witch powers or plain old intuition? I had a second to debate, and then decided I'd answer as honest as possible and see how that worked. "I'm going to see a man about a job."

Looking me over critically, she announced. "You need earrings. I've got some you can borrow. Come with me." Not giving me a chance to argue, she tugged me down the hall to the large back turret room that she shared with her sister. Holly was sound asleep in her bed. Ivy quietly rooted around in her jewelry box for a moment and handed me a pair of amethyst point earrings.

"Those are pretty." I whispered and admired how they seemed to glow in the light.

"Amethyst brings clarity, good luck, and protection against negative magick." Ivy said softly as I put the earrings on.

I had no idea what to say to that, so I murmured my thanks and headed out. As I climbed in the truck, I noticed the gates were open, just like magick. I really had to remember to ask about that one of these days... I programmed the address Duncan had given me into my phone and followed the directions to the house.

I did feel a little guilty about not telling the family that my appointment was with Duncan, but I wanted to gather a little information from some source other than my cousins. I was curious what Duncan would say about this supposed family drama. Meeting him in a public place and outdoors was smart. In the middle of a nice, quiet family neighborhood where people would be around was about as safe as I was liable to get.

A short while later I pulled up in front of a ranch style house that was deep in the throes of rehabbing. I parked my truck and noted the real estate sign in the yard that announced 'Coming Soon!' I wasn't at all surprised to see the agent's name was listed as Rebecca Drake-Quinn.

There was a blue truck in the driveway with the tailgate down. The truck's bed was filled with construction odds and ends and what looked like new shutters. As I climbed out of my truck, I automatically grabbed my notebook and pen and started to jot down impressions as I surveyed the little front yard. It really had potential to be charming. The small yard was neatly divided, almost dead center, by a stone path that came from the driveway and curved up to the front door.

I looked at the yard and let my imagination go a bit until I could see a picture in my mind of a garden layout. Then I fell into my old routine from working with my dad. I took out my cell phone and took a few pictures of the house. For the next few moments I worked quietly.

The front yard of the house was fairly flat. It would be easy to add some colorful perennials and annuals in beds, maybe a crescent shaped flower bed to hug the curve of the flagstone path, and a flowering tree on the side away from the driveway. Excited by the possibilities I started a quick sketch. Adding notes on possible plants and flowers on the side of the paper. I was only interrupted by a friendly, "Good morning," from a very pregnant woman pushing a toddler in a stroller past me on the sidewalk.

The front door to the little house opened and there stood Duncan. The morning sun seemed to illuminate his sandy blonde hair. A tool belt slung low at his hips over khaki cargo shorts. Like me, he had on sturdy boots. To my surprise, he wore a ratty old t-shirt that had seen better days. It was a faded orange, paint splattered, and I could barely make out an old fraternity logo. "Morning." He smiled. He looked harmless, standing there in the doorway of the little house.

I smiled back automatically and felt my heart rap up against my ribs. "Hey," was the best I could manage. I could tell he'd been working for a while, he looked adorably work rumpled, and honestly? Sexy as hell in that tool belt.

While part of me snickered at the idea of a tool belt being sexy, damned if it didn't look good on him. All the dire warnings of my family faded away. I mean seriously... How could anybody who wore old work clothes, worked manual labor, *and* was that good looking, be evil?

For once, I did not want to be at a disadvantage with him. I struggled to act like a professional, and not just stand there and sigh over him. Confidence was my word of the day, I decided. I would be confident no matter what. With that thought in mind, I snapped back to the task at hand.

"Do you have a tape measure I can borrow?" I asked him.

"Sure. Hang on a sec." He disappeared back into the house and was back a moment later. He handed over the tape measure and then held the end for me so I could measure the dimensions of the little front yard. As I jotted down the measurements, he stayed silent and watched.

"Okay, here's what I think would work —" I handed him back the tape measure and proceeded to explain my ideas for the front garden. Then, I moved on to a list of plants. When I finished he grinned at me.

He took the notebook from me and studied the rough sketch. "So, you're not just another pretty face. You do know your stuff."

Stay professional. Be confident, I warned myself. "If

you want me to plant the yard then I will need the names of a few nurseries around here, or if you have an account with one of them you'll need to let me know. I'll go over and see what they have in stock."

He nodded, reached out and snagged my hand, "Okay. Now come take a look at the back yard."

I felt a little tingle when he tugged me along with him in a friendly way, and I had to ask, "Do you always hold hands with your subcontractors?"

"Sure, it gets me a discount." He quipped back.

That made me laugh and we moved to the back yard which was in much better condition than the front. Here a few old trees provided shade and the grass wasn't in too bad of shape. Nothing a little mowing and fertilizer wouldn't cure. He hardly needed my advice here, but he pulled me along to a little deck and sat on the step. He patted the step next to him and since it was quiet and cooler, back in the shade, I sat a step below him. We talked specifics for the planting job for a while, and, I had to admit, I was excited at the prospect of getting my hands in the dirt again.

At least that's what I told myself. How the family would react to my employer was a whole other story. Before this went any further, I needed to get some answers.

"I would love to take the job, but I'll be honest — I'm not sure how my family will react to me working with you." I said.

He scratched his chin. "I take it your aunt has given

you an earful about the families' colorful history?"

"That's one way to put it."

He shrugged. "The old family history isn't of much interest to me. I am more focused on the here and now."

His practical attitude made me feel a little better. "Still, you must have an opinion on the subject?"

"I'm not defined by my family or their particular magickal traditions. It's my own actions that matter. I choose my own path." He said quietly.

The conversation seemed even more otherworldly as we sat in the shade behind the little house. It was quiet, and still, almost expectant. "Duncan, tell me something..."

"Sure."

I had thought about something Aunt Gwen said. So I asked him. "Do you consider yourself an ethical practitioner?"

"I try to be." Duncan leaned back on the step behind him, and seemed totally at ease with the topic of conversation. Then he grinned at me. "So it's my turn to ask — are you a good Witch, Autumn?"

"Well, I hope I am. I'm really new to all of this stuff, I'm still learning."

"I sort of figured that out for myself, after I saw your reaction at the pool a few weeks ago."

"What, do I have..." *What was the term Bran had used?* Then I remembered. "The word 'novice' tattooed on my forehead?"

"No, but you have a very honest and expressive face.

It doesn't hide much." He looked me directly in the eyes and I felt that all the way to my toes. I struggled to act as casually as he did, but I was way out of my league here. So much for my façade of confidence.

Then Duncan caught me off guard, taking my left hand in his. A jolt of power, not entirely pleasant, zipped straight up my arm. It made my fingers tingle. He squeezed lightly in a friendly way, and as I looked up into his face, my stomach did a back flip.

"Here's some more honesty," I began. "I feel a jolt of energy or electricity when we touch. I'm not talking romance novel stuff, I mean energy, and it burns a bit."

"I feel it too." He admitted.

"I've never experienced this before, not even with my father's family. Do you know what it is?"

"It's power. Yours and mine, mingling together." Duncan explained. "Autumn, I don't think it was an accident, us running into each other. I'm wondering if it was fated."

I suppose a comment like that would seem dreamy to some. But after everything I had learned, experienced, and seen in the past few weeks, I was more suspicious, especially with the electrical energy surge that happened when we touched. That energy was still there right now, like a hum right under the surface.

"Fated?" I frowned. "Does that line actually work for you?" I tugged my hand free.

Duncan grinned at me. "I don't suppose you'd believe me if I told you that I have never said that to another woman?"

I gave him a withering look. "What's my open and honest face telling you now?"

Duncan chuckled. "I like you." He sat quietly, no longer touching me. "You can try and read me, if it makes you more comfortable with us working together." He invited.

The thought both excited and worried me at the same time. "The last time I read someone's memories it made them really angry." I told him.

"You can see both the future and the past?"

I thought about it. "Seeing the future is more spontaneous— I don't have much control over it, but reading the past — that's a new trick for me. I can do it, but I have to think about it more and try harder."

He sat there on the little steps of the deck behind the house he was rehabbing and looked totally at ease despite the topic. "I invited you to read me. It won't make me angry. Go ahead."

I was torn between curiosity as to what I would see, and nervousness about trying this with him. Curiosity won. I laid my hand on his arm and let my psychic abilities open up.

And nothing happened. Nothing at all. "I guess I'm nervous." I closed my eyes, concentrated harder and waited. *What the hell?*

A few moments later, I opened my eyes and let go of his arm. Well, this was humiliating. "Sorry. But it didn't work this time. I couldn't pick up anything. Anything at all." I spun away miserably embarrassed, and managed about two steps.

"Hold up." He snagged me by the elbow and turned me to face him. "The last time you read someone's memories, what sort of emotional state were you in?" Duncan asked gently.

"I was angry and frustrated." I admitted.

"You are going to want to watch that." He told me. "Using your powers when you are angry means you'll have no control of the outcome. That's the dark path of magick."

"Which would explain why Aunt Gwen gave me a lecture afterwards." I said half to myself.

"I bet she did." He grinned at that.

And there went Bran's theory of the whole Drake family being evil. Duncan had just warned me to be careful of the dark side — which, come to think of it, sounded a little Star Wars to me.

"Maybe you should try again, but this time you could tap into a more positive emotion." Duncan suggested.

"What, like an experiment?"

"Sure, an experiment —" he said, as he took ahold of both my arms, and kissed me firmly on the mouth.

My purse and notebook hit the ground with a quiet splat, and I automatically gripped his arms back. The second I did, power blasted from the soles of my feet to the top of my head. I could swear I felt my hair blow back, but there was no breeze today. Intrigued, I leaned into him a little more. I felt another surge of power, like his and mine seemed to combine and merge together. It almost felt like we were dancing, even when I knew we were standing still.

His tongue touched mine, and, with a happy sigh, I opened up my mouth fully to his. Then the kiss became more intense. So I hung on and kissed him back.

While I did, dozens of images shifted through my mind: Duncan as a toddler, taking wobbly first steps to his mother's arms. Then, as a young boy riding a bike with a bright green cast on his lower right arm. Duncan as a teenager sitting on the ground with candles in a circle all around him. Next, I saw him with longer hair, working on various old houses, and then I saw his perspective of the first time we literally ran in to each other. He *had* been attracted to me that day. He still was.

This kiss wasn't an experiment at all!

Nope, it's not. Now stop thinking. I clearly heard him think.

My surprise at realizing I could hear his thoughts — and he could hear mine — was soon lost to other sensations. He buried one of his hands in my hair, and pulled me closer still.

Chest to chest, I lost myself in the kiss. With that much body contact, my psychic senses went on overload. To my surprise, I gained a glimpse of his more personal thoughts about me... and what he'd like to do with me. *Oops.*

I pulled back regretfully. "That's enough." I managed. Invited in or not, that sort of intensely personal information seemed unfair, somehow. We stood there our faces inches apart, a little out of breath, arms still around each other. His eyes were open and locked on mine. Then I suddenly remembered we were standing in the middle of an open backyard. Surrounded by family homes, and in plain view of the neighbors.

I took a breath, eased back a bit farther, and tried to calm myself down. "Wow." I finally managed.

He grinned down at me. "That's exactly the response I hope for when I kiss a girl."

I couldn't help it, a laugh bubbled up.

CHAPTER 9

We stood there smiling at each other for a few more moments and then we stepped apart. This changed things. We both knew it, and now we had to decide how to go forward.

"So, did you see anything this time?" Duncan asked quietly as he stood there watching me.

"Yes," I admitted. "One of the images was when you were maybe ten or eleven, riding an old bike with a bright green cast on your right arm." He looked a bit startled so I added, "Broken wrist?"

"I did break my wrist when I was ten. I fell off my —"

"Skateboard," I heard myself say.

Duncan looked at me speculatively. "Autumn, you keep on surprising me."

"I think I surprised myself." I blew out a shaky breath and then picked up my things.

"Don't be afraid of your power."

"I'm not. Not really. But speaking of power... how

did I hear you inside of my head?"

"I have a little telepathy. I can receive and *send* my thoughts every now and then." He shrugged, as if it was no big deal.

"Aunt Gwen picks up on other people's thoughts, but I've noticed she's better at it if she's standing close to them."

"Yeah, the close proximity helps. That's usually how it works for telepaths." He laid his hand on my shoulder, and I felt a little hum of energy.

I rubbed my forehead and tried to process everything. "I get overwhelmed sometimes. There is a lot to learn." I admitted.

"I can help you with that." Duncan made the offer quietly, his expression was sincere.

"Ah..." I fumbled a bit, not sure if that offer held a double meaning.

"Whenever you're ready. No pressure. " He ran a hand down my hair. The gesture was comforting and sweet. "For now, why don't we focus on the landscaping? That way we can get to know each other better."

I nodded in agreement, and, together, we started towards the front yard. "I would like to work with you. On this house, and on the other topic as well."

His blue eyes seemed very intense as he studied me. Now that I had been inside of his head, I wasn't worried about him being evil. I was more worried that I might not be ready for a serious relationship at this point of my life.

"How soon will you want me to get started on the planting?" I asked. It sounded so casual to my own ears that you'd never know we'd just kissed each others brains out.

He played along and went for a casual tone as well. "Most of the construction mess should be cleaned up within two weeks. By then you should be good to start with the flower beds..." Duncan trailed off and then started to chuckle at something.

I had been looking at him while he spoke, but now I swung my head around to see what was so funny. There sat Ivy, perched on the tailgate of Duncan's blue pickup that was parked in the driveway, swinging a leg lazily, as if she had all the time in the world.

"Ivy? What are you doing here?" I sputtered. I wondered how long she had been waiting. And more importantly, had she stayed in the front yard, or had she been around back spying?

"I'm waiting for you." She tipped cat-eye sunglasses down to smile over them. The *Duh,* was unspoken but definitely inferred.

"How's it going?" Duncan laughed over to her.

Ivy jumped lightly down and strolled over to Duncan and me. She looked tough in a black tank, ripped denim shorts, and black combat boots. "So, you really were going to see about a job."

"Do I even want to know how you found me?" I asked.

"Locator spell." Ivy replied smugly, and had Duncan hooting with laughter.

"You did a spell on me?" I was slightly horrified at that idea.

"Didn't have to." Ivy smirked at me.

"Ivy," I said angrily. "Explain. Now."

"The locator spell was on the amethyst earrings you borrowed." She said patiently, "All I had to do was follow those."

"That's fairly ingenious." Duncan said admiringly.

While Ivy grinned at him, I heroically resisted the urge to smack her over the head with my notebook. Tricky Witch. I also made a mental note to never take anything Ivy offered me, even a pair of earrings, ever again.

"Duncan," I said seriously. "I think the first thing you should teach me, magick-wise, is how to know if an item has been spelled by my family, or not."

He agreed that it was probably a good idea.

As if to placate me, Ivy held up her hands. "Before you get all pissy... I stayed out here. I did *not* invade your privacy. I only wanted to check and make sure you were okay."

"I don't need a damn bodyguard." I told her. "I can take care of myself." I took the earrings off and handed them to Ivy.

Duncan shook his head at her, and went to get a set of shutters out of the bed of the truck. Ivy grabbed a second set and followed him as he moved to the front porch, probably trying to make up for her behavior.

"Look, I get that you guys like each other. But the family is going to be dead set against it." Ivy warned.

Duncan shrugged, "That's their problem." He told her and took the shutters.

"Well for what it's worth," Ivy said seriously to him. "I think you're probably okay."

Torn between anger and amazement at her audacity, I literally slapped my hand to my forehead. I shook my head at her and caught Duncan's eye, it appeared he was amused by her antics and not angry at all. Well, that was something, I supposed.

Apparently comfortable with her own nosiness, Ivy stuck her head inside the open door of the house and looked around. "I love rehabbing projects. Why don't you show me what you're doing here?" Ivy fairly radiated good cheer as she stood there, which was why Duncan ended up giving us a tour of the house.

As we walked through the bright, open rooms of the home, Ivy fired off questions to Duncan about original hardwood floors and granite versus composite material countertops. It made me appreciate, as I listened to her, how much she really was into this. When she hunkered down to look at the tile Duncan had chosen for the bathroom, he seemed to genuinely enjoy her enthusiasm for renovations.

We were standing on the front porch again when I spotted the same woman I had seen earlier, walking slowly back down the sidewalk in front of the house.

She was eyeballing it, I knew intuitively, and she wanted it for her own. "I think you have a prospective buyer out there." I motioned towards the woman and the stroller.

Duncan went to go speak to her, which left me alone with Ivy.

"Listen, *Sabrina* —" I began as soon as Duncan was out of earshot.

"That's me, a teenage Witch for sure. Tragically I'm not blonde. I do have a black cat though —" Ivy quipped.

"Try and focus Ivy!" I snapped. "Spying on me is not cool. Seriously, what the hell were you thinking?"

"Sorry, I only wanted to make sure you were okay." She shrugged.

"It may shock you to know that I can take care of myself. I have been doing it for years." I informed her.

"But you have no defenses and hardly any experience when it comes to magick." Ivy pointed out.

I went on the offensive. "Well, that's because your mother won't teach me any magick! So far it's all grounding and centering and rules." I groused.

"Yeah, I always hated that too." Ivy agreed. She scuffed her boot on the porch and looked down at the ground. "Tell you what," Ivy said brightening. "How about I teach you that locator spell?"

"Here comes Duncan, hold that thought." I suggested.

"You were right; she is interested in the house."

Duncan announced. "I told her it should be ready by the end of the month. That is, if I can get back on schedule."

Which was our clue to leave. Duncan gave me the name of the nursery where he had an account. Ivy announced she would give me directions so we could go straight there.

"Great. I'll see you two later then." Duncan shut my door for me.

"Wait, what do you mean, you two?" I asked.

"I can always use another set of hands to clean up and gopher around here." Duncan looked meaningfully at Ivy, who blew her cool image and squealed in excitement.

Her eyes lit up. "I'll do anything! Grout tile, sand the floors—"

"Clean up and run errands." Duncan corrected. "After school a couple of days, and on Saturdays. Minimum wage, to start. We'll see how you do and go from there."

"Thanks Duncan!" Ivy bounced on the seat all smiles.

"You're sure about this?" I asked him — meaning Ivy.

"You're hired." Duncan said. "The both of you."

***

To my surprise, I enjoyed going plant shopping with

Ivy. As I walked through the garden center, notebook in hand, plotting and calculating, she was attentive and flagged every plant I picked out with the neon green plant tags the nursery owner had given me. With a promise from the owner to set all of my chosen items aside, we left, grabbed some fast food, and headed for the riverfront park to eat our lunch under the shade of an old willow.

"So," Ivy said around a mouth full of sub sandwich. "How about I teach you some magick?"

I sputtered and almost spit my soda out; whipping my head around to make sure no one was close enough to overhear her.

"Relax." Ivy rolled her eyes at me. "If you haven't noticed, people are giving us plenty of privacy."

Come to think of it, people were avoiding the area. "Why is that?" I asked.

"I put a *reluctance* on the area around the willow tree." Ivy made a broad circular gesture with both hands.

"Say what?"

"A reluctance." Ivy explained. "It's a type of magick that makes people—"

"Reluctant!" I got it.

"Right. Reluctant to come close to a place, person, or thing." She finished.

"How's that work?" Now she had my attention.

"You work with the natural energy that is present, the four natural elements of earth, air, fire, and water, and then you give other people in the area a little energetic nudge to stay away."

I considered that. "Wouldn't that be manipulative?" According to the lectures from Gwen, magickal manipulation was bad.

"Well..." Ivy drew the word out. "There's manipulation, and then there's a little encouragement."

"That's like saying six to one, half dozen to the other." I argued.

"No, it's all in the intention." Ivy explained. "If your intention is to create a private or a hidden sacred space, that is acceptable. The spell would make folks reluctant to disturb you or the area. The same thing would apply to hiding something valuable. As in making folks look past what is right in front of them."

I set my sandwich aside and mulled that over. "Could you use a reluctance on the last sweater in your size at the store? So that come payday it would still be there waiting for you?"

Warming to the topic, Ivy leaned forward. "That falls in the category of gray magick. You know, not white as in positive, and not black as in baneful."

I knew that term. "Baneful is an old term for poisonous or deadly."

"How'd you know that?" Ivy asked clearly surprised.

"My dad taught me." I said softly and wondered.

"Autumn, have you ever considered that maybe your dad taught you more than you realized? I've heard you mention faery stories and mythology that your dad told you about. And I bet when he taught you about plants, you learned more than just their botanical names."

Stunned, I only sat there. "I never thought about that."

"You know I wonder..." Ivy stood up and walked around behind me, holding her hands above my head.

"Ivy!" I squealed, torn between embarrassment and laughter. "People are gonna wonder what you are doing."

"Hello. Reluctance, remember?" She waved away my concern. "They won't see a thing. I just want to see what your personal energy feels like."

"Why are you checking my aura?" I asked suspiciously as she held her hands a few inches above my head and slowly passed them down and over my shoulders and back.

"I'm checking you for spells." Ivy explained. "Now shut the hell up and let me concentrate." She ordered.

"Whoa! Hold on there Sabrina!" I started to jump up, and Ivy shoved me back to the grass. "Why would I have spells on me?" I wanted to know.

"Tell you what." Ivy said, "If you let me do this, I'll teach you how to check to see if any item, or person, has been spelled."

I considered that. "Deal." I agreed, and stayed seated.

Ivy patted the top of my head. After a moment of her standing back there, she sat down directly across from me. She crossed her legs and our knees bumped. I set my soda down and Ivy grabbed both my hands. "Okay, hang on cousin." She gave my hands a squeeze and then announced, "Here we go."

Hearing that, I squeezed my eyes shut, and braced for the worst. Instead, what I felt was a gentle current pass from Ivy to me. And then from me, back to my cousin. Curious, I opened my eyes and looked to see what Ivy was doing.

Her hair ruffled around her face on what I assumed was a breeze, but I had a moment of clarity when I noticed that nothing else was moving. Not the draping branches of the willow we sat under, not our clothes, not my hair. It wasn't a breeze that caused the movement of Ivy's hair. It was power. Her power.

My heart thudded hard in my chest and I gulped. Ivy's grip tightened. Her eyes opened and met mine. A light was in them similar to the light I had seen shine from Bran's that night when he built the energy ball.

"Well, hello there." Ivy said softly as if she were seeing something unexpected.

"What?" I asked her slightly alarmed.

"There *is* an old spell on you. It's a cross between a reluctance and a muffling spell. It's maybe twenty years old. So it's worn thin." Ivy said very matter of fact.

My mind raced as to how she knew that, and also how I knew absolutely that she was right. She squeezed my hands again, and I looked back in her eyes. "It's been on me since I was a little girl?" *Who the hell would have put a spell on me when I was little?* "Let's get this off me then!"

"We can break it." Ivy announced, eyebrows raised. She flashed me a smile that was all determination. "Follow my lead, cousin."

Ivy quietly told me that I would need to imagine building up my personal energy, my power, and having it shine bright and out from my heart. Then, she told me to visualize the old spell as a cracked egg shell. A shell that wrapped around my chest and back. I took a deep breath, closed my eyes, and concentrated. After a few moments, Ivy told me to open my eyes and look.

When I looked down, to my surprise, I saw a slight pink glow radiating out from my body. I gasped and told Ivy what I was seeing.

"That's your energy. Don't be afraid, it's a part of you after all." Ivy explained. "Push it out harder now, make it shine brighter and repeat after me."

I nodded and visualized what she told me. I also reminded myself that I had wanted to learn about magick, after all. So I had better Witch the hell up and not back down now. "I'm ready." I said grimly.

Ivy began to chant, "We seek now to break, what was once cast. By the elements four, this clearing will last."

I repeated after Ivy quietly, and felt my chest and back muscles tighten up. The pressure wasn't horrible, but it wasn't comfortable either.

Ivy continued. "Whether cast with love, or with an

intent to harm, the old spell will shatter as we both speak this charm."

I repeated, "Whether cast with love, or an intent to harm," and the tightness became unbearable. Gasping, I gripped Ivy's hands and pushed through it. "The old spell will shatter as we both speak this charm!"

The shell seemed to explode and it sounded like glass shattering. Suddenly I could breathe easily again, and I felt about ten pounds lighter. I looked at my cousin, and tears started to well up.

"You kicked ass, Autumn!" Ivy said proudly, and she grabbed me up in a fierce hug that lifted me to my knees. We knelt there under the willow tree, hanging on to each other, and laughing like lunatics. "By all the power of three times three..." Ivy began and pulled back to grin at me.

I nodded. I knew what to do to close the spell. "As we will it, so shall it be!" I said proudly. With that, a breeze came sweeping through, and all of the draping branches of the willow whipped back and forth. "This is amazing!" I managed, and climbed to my feet, as my hair streamed back from my face, and much cooler air blew in.

As we watched, clouds billowed up from the west, and a rumble of thunder sounded in the distance. A little drunk on the rush of power, I raised my hands in the air and shouted. Ivy slung an arm around my waist, and we stood there and watched as the cold front came roaring in.

I felt incredible, I felt invincible, and I felt like nothing would ever be the same for me again. And then suddenly I felt light headed. "Um, Ivy..." I managed, as my knees began to wobble.

"Oops. Sit your butt down." Ivy directed.

I quickly sat on the grass, and put my head between my knees. "What happened?" I managed.

"What goes up must come back down." Ivy said as she sat next to me. "Eat something," she suggested. "You just used a hell of a lot of magickal energy."

I grabbed my half eaten sandwich and devoured it, as Ivy explained to me that magickal energy, like physical energy, came at a cost. If you expend any kind of energy, then you will have to re-fuel. Kindly, Ivy passed me the other half of her sandwich and I scarfed that down too.

After a while, I started to feel steadier, but I sure didn't want to jump up and do anything physical. "I think I'm going to need a nap." I told her as I finished off my soda.

"That's not a bad idea, actually." Ivy agreed. "You do realize that you probably called that storm in?"

I'm sure my eyes bugged right out of my head. "What?" I asked, incredulous. As if on cue a few drops of rain started to fall. "I... I... but I didn't mean to." I stuttered.

"Bet mom's gonna be pissed." Ivy leaned back on her elbows in the grass and smiled up at the light rain. She seemed very nonchalant about the whole affair.

"Don't worry though. Once she gets over that, she'll be proud of you for blowing through that old spell."

As if that was going to make it all better? I followed her lead and lay down in the grass. I felt better immediately. As soon as my back hit the earth, I felt steadier. "Are we grounding and centering?" I asked her.

"Yes, my young apprentice." Ivy snarked back.

I laughed, and we lay there, under the old willow, and listened to the rain fall. Occasionally a few drops made their way through, but it felt so great with that cooler breeze. Who cared about a little rain?

"Ivy?" I asked her a little while later.

"Yeah?"

"You called that old spell we broke, a reluctance and a muffling type of spell?"

Ivy sat up. "Yeah, that's the best way I can think to describe it."

I sat slowly up as well and started to gather the remains of our lunch. "Why would someone do that to me?"

Before I could ask anything else, Aunt Gwen walked through the draping branches of the willow trees. "Hello girls." She said quietly, and she did not look happy.

"Oh shit." Ivy and I said in unison.

CHAPTER 10

"Before you start to yell," Ivy said. "Let me explain. —"

"One of you had better." Gwen warned, as she stood, glowering, under a black umbrella.

I glanced over at Ivy and she tossed me a look that said, *Let me handle this.* I wasn't sure if I should try and help or scramble behind the trunk of the willow tree to get out of the line of fire.

To my surprise, Gwen didn't launch into a lecture. Instead, she closed the umbrella with a snap, and sat neatly on the ground between the two of us, clearly peeved. "Spill it." She told her daughter.

And boy did she. Ivy started at when she loaned me the earrings, to her waiting for me at the house, the job offer, our nursery trip, and then to performing magick under the old willow. "Mom, there was a spell on Autumn." Ivy confided.

Gwen balked at the news about the job, but her eyes narrowed speculatively over the news about the spell,

"Do you know what sort of spell?"

"It felt like a reluctance and a muffling spell, all wrapped up into one." Ivy explained.

Gwen seemed to consider that. Then her eyes met mine. "I'll be honest. I've wondered for some time if your abilities were bound."

I had stayed silent during their exchange, but now I spoke up. "Bound? Who would do that to me?" As soon as I said it, I *knew*. My heart broke a little. "My father?"

"I believe so." Gwen said gently.

"But why?" I asked Gwen.

"There is no way for me to be sure." Gwen admitted. "But if I had to guess, I'd say he did it to placate your mother. Often powers manifest when a child is going through puberty, but magickal talents can appear earlier. If you were displaying powers early... "

"Then he muffled, or bound them." It made sense. My mother always had been terrified of anything to do with the occult, or even New Age topics. It also explained why she had been so unhappy with my decision to move here and go to grad school. I recalled her melodramatic goodbye speech she had made when I was leaving. *If you choose this path over your own mother, then you will never be allowed in my home again...*

Gwen rose up. "Show me where you were when you broke the spell."

I got to my feet and showed her approximately where Ivy and I had been sitting. As I watched, Gwen hunkered down in the spot, and held her left hand out over the ground. She swept it back and forth a few times. Now, she turned to me with her hand held out. I helped her up.

"May I?" She asked. I gave my consent and she also ran her hands above my head and over my shoulders.

I felt something pop in my back, and I grunted. "What was that?"

"A little energetic shard of that old spell that was left behind." She explained. "You are clear of it now." Gwen looked at her daughter, "That was an impressive bit of casting, Ivy."

"It wasn't all me." Ivy grinned and stood next to me. "Autumn, did most of it." The pride in her voice almost made me blush.

"Which one of you called the storm?" Gwen wanted to know. She seemed calmer now, almost resigned.

"I did." I said.

"That was an accident." Ivy said in my defense.

I rubbed my temple, where a headache had started to brew. "Would it help if I said that I didn't mean to and don't even know how it was possible?"

Gwen sighed. "So you want to learn more magick?"

"Yes, I do."

"You'll have to find time between your classes and this landscaping job you took on." Her tone was serious, as was her expression.

"I'll make the time."

Gwen smiled at me slowly, but it wasn't exactly

comforting. "It's going to be intense training. I won't go easy on you."

"Bring it on." I said and matched her tone.

"Holly and I can help teach her. It'll be fun!" Ivy laughed. "Let's do something now!" Ivy suggested and scampered out from under the willow branches and towards the walking path in the park.

"I want you to be very careful working with Duncan Quinn." Gwen warned me quietly. "His family is not to be trusted, no matter how nice he may seem. There is a lot of hate directed at us from that family."

"Would you feel better if I told you that he invited me to read him?" I made direct eye contact with my aunt. "He also warned me that I shouldn't use my abilities when I was angry, to be careful because that leads to a dark path."

"He cautioned you about the dark path, *and* he let you read him?" Gwen seemed surprised.

"Yes Ma'am, he did. And I did read him." I confirmed.

"Well, I never would have expected that." Gwen seemed dumbfounded as she mulled over that bit of information. Our conversation was cut short when Ivy came back, slightly soaked from the rain and holding two pebbles, one in each hand.

"One is spelled the other is not," Ivy announced. "Figure out which is which."

I gazed thoughtfully at the pebbles. Visually they were unremarkable. I held my right hand over them palm down.

Gwen stopped me by saying. "Use your receptive hand to receive impressions. The receptive hand is opposite of your writing hand, so for you — that's your left."

I switched hands and tried that. When my left hand touched Ivy's hand, I got a flash of her choosing the stones and saying a quick chant. But I couldn't tell which particular one was spelled. So my postcognitive ability showed me the how but not the particulars. I told Gwen that and wondered what to do next. She only raised an eyebrow, but said nothing.

Okay, so Witch school is in session. And Gwen wasn't kidding about the not going easy on me thing. I considered trying a quick charm, but I didn't know any. Could I simply make one up myself? I had accidentally called in a storm front, so I ought to be able to do this...

I shook out both my hands and focused on the pebbles that Ivy held. I thought about the four elements. They were all present. I was standing under a tree and on the ground, so there was the earth. Air was obviously all around us. Fire... well maybe I could think of the sun for my fire. And water, dripped down through the willow branches from the rain. In my mind, I pictured them lending me their strength and support.

An idea for a charm popped into my head, and I quietly chanted. "What was cast in secret, is now revealed to me. As I will it, so mote it be." Immediately one of the pebbles started to glow with a soft purple light. As I watched, a Rune appeared on the pebble in Ivy's right hand.

"Hey that's really good!" Ivy said.

"Where'd you learn that charm?" Gwen wanted to know.

"I made it up, I just improvised it." I admitted.

As I watched, the little Rune faded away. Ivy brought her hands to her mouth and blew across the pebbles. It looked like the bit of magick was gone. Then, she cheerfully chucked them out back on the path where she found them.

Gwen stood there, looking at me with a serious expression. "You really made that charm up spontaneously?"

"Yeah, was that okay?" I asked her.

"What's your schedule for the rest of the day?" Gwen asked me.

A little caught off guard, I answered. "I don't have anything going on."

"You do now." Gwen announced. "Girls, gather your things. We are heading back to the shop. Ivy, you've got the counter for the afternoon. Autumn and I are going to start training. Immediately."

"Please tell me I'm not going to be doing that in the middle of the store, in front of the customers." I grimaced as we stepped out from under the sheltering willow.

Gwen pushed the button on her umbrella handle and it snapped open, just like magick. "Well, of course not.

We will use the class room space in the back."

Ivy and I scurried back to my truck and Gwen walked behind us, casually with her umbrella. The rain was really coming down now, so Ivy and I quickly got into the truck and waited for Gwen.

"You impressed her." Ivy confided to me.

"Really?" I wiped the rain out of my eyes, and considered that.

"Yeah, otherwise you would have gotten a top volume lecture." Ivy pulled a large bandana out of her pocket and offered it to me. "Tell you more later." She said as Gwen joined us.

***

Magick, it turns out is a hell of a lot of work. I mean, who knew? Apparently I had gotten lucky, using a combination of postcognition and an impromptu 'find the spelled pebble' charm in the park, because for the rest of the day Gwen busted my ass, and nothing came as easily as that first charm. By the time she finished with me on Saturday, I was worn out. I now had an impressive list of magickal books to read, a massive amount of correspondences to memorize, and a quiz to look forward to at the end of the week. Seriously. A quiz.

According to my aunt, raw talent and luck were one thing, but discipline, training, study and practice was what would yield me dependable results. I was a good

Witch student and threw myself into it. After a few days I saw a little improvement, and that kept me motivated to squeeze in Craft studies between my grad school studying.

The following Friday, I was back on campus with *another* huge reading list, this time from my Introduction to Museum Studies class. I had left my afternoon class and went straight to the university library, wanting to get some studying in before I broke ground at Duncan's rehabbed house the next day. The weather was much cooler now, and to celebrate I strolled into the library wearing my favorite boots, old jeans, and a new persimmon colored sweater. According to my Craft studies, orange was a color that promoted vitality. Whether it was color magick or not, the new sweater did make me feel a little sassy. I saw Bran working behind the reference desk when I entered the library, and he'd deigned to give me a nod.

The pompous ass. Just when I thought he might be coming around. The news of my working with Duncan had puckered him right up again. I resisted the urge to sneer at him, and instead, as I was a more superior, highly evolved being, I waited until I was in the stacks to do so.

Despite being in my cousin's domain, I had to admit that the university library had a great atmosphere. Lots of dark wood trim and pretty old fashioned green study lamps were at each table. I found a quiet table, sat down with my stack of books, legal pad, and pens. I adjusted the little lamp, got out my laptop, and happily worked on my assignments.

I'd been working for maybe an hour, the comings and goings of the other students didn't disturb me, I was used to studying in libraries. I flagged a few pages to copy out of the best reference book of the lot, and noticed that someone was standing across the table from me.

Not only standing, but rudely staring, was a man maybe in his early sixties. He had salt and pepper hair that receded back in a widow's peak. He wore an expensive looking grey pin striped suit, and his eyes were unfriendly and dark. He could have been an attractive older man, but he stared down at me like I was an interesting bug he'd unfortunately happened to come across.

As I met his eyes, I swear I felt the temperature drop in the library. I felt defensive and belligerent from the way he was looking me over. Since the man might have been faculty at the University, instead of saying something sarcastic, I asked politely, "Is there a problem?"

The man scoffed, pulled out a chair, and sat uninvited, directly across from me. He took his time smoothing out his slacks after he sat, and then folded his hands on the table top. He gave me a look that was challenging and a little intimidating.

"You're Autumn Bishop." He said quietly.

"Yes. And you are?"

"Thomas Drake." He introduced himself, and, even though his voice was quiet, the words seemed to make an emotional impact square in the middle of my chest. This was Duncan's uncle, and his creepy cousin Julian's father.

I didn't say it was nice to meet him, because I had a really, really bad feeling about this. I may be new to the whole witchcraft thing, but I could feel bad vibes coming off of him. *This* was the person that had my father's family in such a snit. And after spending only a moment in his presence, I was starting to understand why.

"So, you are going to be working with my nephew now? Planting flowers, I believe?" His voice was fluid and elegantly disdainful, and made me want to get away from him as quickly as possible.

With a sudden insight, I knew that this man was used to getting his own way, by whatever means necessary. It also became very clear, as he smirked at me, that Thomas Drake was trying to intimidate me. Showing weakness would be a very bad idea. So instead of bolting, I folded my arms and rested them on the desk as I considered how to best handle him.

"What can I do for you, Mr. Drake?" I bluffed, and acted as if I was bored.

"Right this moment? Not a thing. But I do have plans for you and your psychic abilities in the very near future." He said with a slight smile.

I felt my skin crawl and worked hard not to recoil

from him, because, jeez, this guy was creepy as shit. "Not interested." I told him as I picked up my pen and acted as if I was going to finish taking notes out of the library books.

"My dear, the things I could teach you... there is so much more to our world than you know."

"Pass." I said straight faced and in a bored tone.

His laugh was low, and seriously made me think of a movie villain. "You have courage." He stated. "I like that." His tone was seductive, and made my stomach heave.

Yeah, and that was *way* more than enough. I started to scan the area to see how many other people were close by, since I might need to call for help. Embarrassing as that might have been, I would bet that a man like Drake would not want to cause a scene in public. But as I looked around, I saw that no one was in my immediate area. And there should have been. The library had been full of students a while ago. Students studying, working on their laptops, and browsing the stacks. That was weird. Where did everyone go?

He used a reluctance. I realized and my heart started to beat faster. He had spelled the area to keep people away so he could talk to me. I focused and looked at him, hard. The room behind him looked slightly out of focus and the normal background noises of the library were muted, almost like we were under a big glass dome.

"Nice reluctance." I said in an off hand tone. "Kind

of overkill for a public place though." I shrugged, like it was nothing of importance, but my muscles were coiled and I shifted in my chair, ready to move quickly, should it become necessary.

"You are much more like Gwen than Arthur. Your aunt, she has courage. Your father, unfortunately... was a coward."

Fear disappeared. I pushed up to my feet, leaned over the table and into his personal space. "You know *nothing* about my father."

He glanced up at me unconcerned, "Sit down." He suggested, and calmly flicked his hand in my direction — and I found myself sitting.

I blinked in confusion. *How the hell did he do that?* I tried to move, and discovered that I couldn't.

"I admire your spirit." He seemed almost pleased with me, and he leaned back in his chair totally relaxed. "My dear, your father ran from this town with your Cowan mother over twenty years ago. He turned his back on his legacy, his blood, and then he obviously bound your powers. Those are the actions of a coward." Drake explained almost patiently. He brushed lint off his jacket sleeve and then added. "By the way, how did any of that work out for you?"

My butt may have been stuck to the chair, but my brain and mouth were still working just fine. "Listen Slick," I said. "I'm not sure what you are trying to prove with this little power play, but even I know you can't hold this forever."

"If I could please have a moment of your undivided attention." Thomas said and snapped his fingers under my nose.

I yanked my head back and then felt a pressure squeeze tight around my chest. It hurt to move. It hurt to breathe. He certainly had my attention now.

"Your father took something that belonged to me, twenty two years ago. A grimoire. It's called the Blood Moon Grimoire. It is an antique book, bound in dark red leather. I want you to retrieve it and bring it back to me." His eyes were intense as he spoke.

He snapped his fingers again and the pressure let up. I gasped for air and started struggling again. "If you know that he bound my powers, what makes you think he would have given an old spell book to me?" I tried to ask and catch my breath, all at the same time.

Thomas Drake ignored my attempts to move and leaned in a little closer across the library table. "You will retrieve the Blood Moon Grimoire and bring it to me before the next full moon, or there will be consequences."

"What do you mean consequences?" I asked. *What did that give me, less than three weeks?*

"I believe you had a close call not too long ago. A SUV that ran a stop sign?"

I blinked. "Are you admitting that was you?"

"I am merely pointing out that accidents happen. Your twin cousins, they're lovely young girls. It would certainly be a shame for you to loose yet another family member." He said in a quiet, matter of fact way, that I admit scared me right down to my toes.

As he laughed quietly at my dismay, I began to concentrate on trying to reach Bran using my psychic abilities. I couldn't physically touch my cousin this time, but damn it — he was close by. He worked in the freaking library. I should be able to contact him somehow... Come on, The Sight, don't let me down. *Bran, I need help!* I aimed my thoughts at where I had last seen him, and sent him a mental image. *Get your ass over here!*

I was starting to feel a little desperate. Sweat slid down my back and I was *way* the hell out of my league. I tried to tamp down my fear, struggled to reproduce the energy I had used over the weekend, and break free of the spell all at the same time.

"Relax, my dear." Thomas Drake suggested with a little sigh. "Don't waste your power trying to weaken my spell. Instead, I suggest that you use those abilities to locate the Blood Moon Grimoire."

"I am not your dear." I panted and worked harder, then was rewarded for my effort. As I saw for the first time since Drake had stood over my library table, a person walked through the stacks. Normal background noises started to trickle through as well. *The spell was fading!* I pushed out from my gut with everything I had, and then I felt one of my legs move.

Suddenly with a loud crash, Bran appeared and ran a large library cart full of books straight into my table.

Books went tumbling and Thomas Drake jolted from the impact. The noise had been jarring, and it sounded even louder in the typical quiet of the library.

I jumped to my feet, while Bran stalked around the cart and grabbed Thomas Drake by the lapels of his suit coat. He hauled him to his feet in a smooth motion that had me blinking. "Let me help you out, sir." Bran sounded perfectly polite, but the expression was murderous.

Thomas Drake only smiled at Bran, which scared the crap out of me, and made Bran yank the older man up to his toes.

"Bran..." I warned him.

My cousin never even spared me a look. He leaned into Thomas Drake's face a bit more, and practically growled. "Stay away from my family." As if to punctuate the warning, the little green study lamp on the table popped loudly and went out.

"Are we finished with the theatrics, boy?" Drake asked, way too pleasantly.

Bran released his hold on Thomas Drake, and Drake stepped back from my cousin, brushing lazily at the lapels of his now wrinkled suit.

"Get out." Bran's voice was quiet, but the threat was crystal clear.

Thomas Drake stepped around the library cart and stopped to study the two of us. "I do hate to leave, however I have an appointment. Besides, the two of you have much to discuss. What with your *close* family connections, and so forth." Thomas sneered at us, clearly implying something. Though I didn't understand, I watched Bran's face turn dark red.

I had a moment to wonder about that, before Thomas Drake smiled at me, "I truly enjoyed meeting you, my dear, I'll look forward to seeing you again soon." Then he nodded to Bran and sauntered away, all cocky and casual like he was off to the club or something. Bastard.

After he was gone, I let out a long shaky breath. "You got my psychic message?" I asked quietly. Now that the spell was broken, people were once again walking around us and a few were staring at the mess that the book cart crash had caused.

"I did." Bran started to pick up the scattered books from the cart.

I couldn't think of what to do next, so I grabbed a few of the books that had fallen on my side of the table. I handed them to Bran and our hands touched.

Bran ignored the offered books, and wrapped his fingers around my wrist. "Are you okay?" He looked at me intently. "Did he touch you?" His voice was library quiet, but Bran's expression was intense.

"No, not physically. But he did do magick on me." I admitted. I quietly relayed to Bran what had happened. When I told him about Drake's threat against the twins, another lamp blew out with a soft pop, on a nearby study table. "Easy there, Sparky." I warned him. "I'm okay, thanks to you. But I think you need to rein your powers in."

Bran closed his eyes, and I could see him struggle for control. While he did, I watched, fascinated, as the overhead lights flickered. A few seconds later the flickering stopped, and he opened his eyes, and seemed to be his typical self. "Are you finished studying for the day?" He asked, still holding onto my wrist.

"Well, I could stand to put in a few more hours. And that asshole is not going to make me run from the library like a scared little girl." I told Bran.

Bran gave my hand a little squeeze and then took the books from me. "Fine, but you are going to study in my office until you are ready to leave. Gather your things, and follow me." Bran ordered.

I started to protest, then thought better of it. "Okay." I scooped up what I could, and to my surprise Bran gathered the rest. I followed him to his office at the library, and he set me up to work at his desk.

"Stay here, but leave the door open. When you are ready to leave, text me, and I will walk you out myself." He ordered. I saw him reach for his cell phone as he left and figured he'd be contacting the family. A couple of days ago I would have sneered at that idea of an escort to my truck. However, there was nothing like an up close and personal with a creepy dark magician to make you appreciate the depths of your own vulnerability.

I did my best to get back to work, and I felt safer in Bran's tidy little office. I discovered a big chunk of amethyst on his desk that he seemed to be using as a paperweight. I'd read up more on amethyst after Ivy had lent me the spelled earrings. Amethyst was an extremely powerful and protective stone. It also had calming properties and helped reduce stress. I ran my fingers over it, hoping the stone would work its magick —because boy I needed some stress reduction— and replayed what had just happened in my mind. The effortless way that Drake had spelled me into that chair and damn near cut off my air while I sat there helpless... There was no denying it. This incident had shaken me.

Not to mention Thomas Drake's comments about my father being a coward. I definitely had to find out more about that — And what was all this soap opera intrigue about a Blood Moon Grimoire? He thought that my father had stolen it, and that *I* knew where it was? I gave up studying, put my head in my hands, and tried to process everything that had happened.

I recalled all of the warnings Gwen and Bran had given me about the Drake family, and now I knew that they had not been over exaggerating. Not at all. For about a half hour I tried to settle down and get back in to my studies. Then my cell phone started to blow up with text messages from Gwen and the girls.

They were all checking on me, Gwen announced she would be at home waiting for me. Holly's message was sympathetic and sweet, and Ivy's simply said: **I'm going to release the flying monkeys!!**

That made me laugh, and, as I answered them all back, I started to feel a bit better. I soon gave up studying for the rest of the afternoon as a lost cause. I sent Bran a text and let him know I was ready to go, stacked up my books, and shut down my laptop.

Bran did walk me to my truck. He suggested that I drive straight home and I only nodded in reply. I pulled out of the University and made my way back through town, my mind racing with everything that had happened. I told myself to relax and to enjoy the pretty tree lined streets, but it was almost impossible. I pulled to a stop at an intersection and waited for a pedestrian to cross. When they didn't seem inclined to, I glanced over.

And found myself looking at the ghost of that police officer.

I whipped the truck to the curb and hopped out. Before I even realized my intention, I was out on the sidewalk and marching right up to him. "What the hell do you want?" I demanded.

His pleasant face seemed almost familiar, and I found the air chilled considerably the closer I got. I stopped a few feet away from him when he simply held up a hand. "Are you alright?" He asked me.

Later I would think back and wonder that I didn't even worry that someone might drive by and see me talking to thin air, but at that moment I was too wound up and frustrated to care. "Why are you haunting me?" I asked.

For a second his image wavered and then became true. "You need my help, and I need yours."

"Who are you?"

His image rippled and he sounded farther away. "A friend."

A breeze whipped through, and all of the leaves on the trees shook and trembled above us. "But I don't — didn't know you." I corrected myself.

"Your father did." Was his answer, and it caused all of the hair to rise up of the back of my neck. Then he started to fade away.

"Hey! Wait!" I protested.

"Look to the past to save someone in the future." His voice and form became transparent, and then he was gone. Again.

Dumbfounded I stood there for a moment and waited to see if he would reappear. When he didn't, I stalked back to my truck and slammed the door behind myself. I sat in the cab and shook in reaction. So this ghost had known my father. Okay, that was one bit of information I didn't have before. But the comment he made at the end of his visit, I did not understand.

Before I could forget it, I grabbed my smart phone, hit the Notes app, and spoke. "He said, 'Look to the past to save someone in the future.'" I hit save and looked over the text. That seemed right. But as to what that meant, I had no clue.

I tried to pull myself together and to think clearly. I made another note in my phone to do some research and to see if a local officer had died recently. But what connected these two visitations? I put my phone away and thought it over. This was the second time I had 'spoken' to the ghost. At my first encounter he had told me to 'be safe.' Today he asked if I was alright.

My stomach dropped as I recalled that the first time he had spoken to me, it had been after the close call with the black SUV that ran the stop sign. Today I'd had a personal encounter with Thomas Drake, who had all but admitted he was involved in that almost-collision, and now the ghost appeared again. Clearly he was concerned for my safety. And that realization made me break out in goose bumps.

Resolved, I drove carefully back to the manor. I needed answers, and I knew who would probably have them. Gwen.

CHAPTER 11

Still wound up from the encounter in the library and the second ghostly visit, I stomped up the porch steps and shoved open the front door of the manor house. Holly and Ivy were sitting on the dark stained steps of the main staircase. Merlin sat a step above them and watched me with unblinking golden eyes. I didn't even get the chance to put my things down before they all pounced.

I held up a hand to stop their rapid fire questions, explaining that I'd rather tell the story only once. I scooped up Merlin for some kitty comfort, and we walked into the family room together. I really liked this room. It was relaxing and comfortable in a sort of shabby chic way, with a cheerful mixture of antiques and traditional furniture.

I stopped short, and was surprised to see a few vintage wooden crates and several large pots of live chrysanthemums in orange and gold sitting by the fireplace. A storage box filled with garlands of colorful leaves and a variety of other fall items, sat nearby. *I guess my little magickal emergency had tragically interrupted the family's seasonal decorating.*

I cringed at my internal monologue and told myself to stop being bitchy. I must have been more wound up than I thought.

"What's all this?" I made a real effort to sound polite, and gestured to the box as I chose an oversized, cushy chair close to the fireplace, while the girls shouted to Gwen that I was home. Merlin deigned to sit on the arm of the chair next to me, and, with a sigh, I settled in. I felt the last of the adrenalin fade away, and my stomach took a nasty turn. I closed my eyes and pressed a hand to it.

"We are going to start decorating for the sabbat." Holly explained. "The autumn equinox, is next week. That is one of eight sabbats, or holy days, in the Witch's year."

The sabbats were on my list of witch homework from Gwen, I recalled, as I made myself focus on something besides the drama of the day and my queasy stomach. It had been a weird sort of surprise to discover that this year the sabbat and my birthday fell on the same day.

Gwen came in a moment later with a cup of tea and a little plate of sugar cookies. "This will fix you right up." She calmly handed me the tea, which smelled like peppermint, and set the cookies down on a side table within my reach.

"Thanks." I said, and I reached carefully for the cup with both hands, as mine had started to shake.

"You will need to build back up your blood sugar levels after a magickal attack *and* expending all that energy." She explained, as I sipped the tea slowly. I waited a bit to see how my stomach would react, and, sure enough, the tea did seem to soothe it.

Gwen hovered for a moment and then settled on the sofa across from me. The twins sat as one on the area rug and gave me their full attention. I nibbled on a cookie and felt a little better. As I told them about my encounter with Thomas Drake, I watched Gwen's eye's narrow. I noted that Ivy and Holly gasped when I used the word "Cowan." Apparently that was a really nasty word for non magickal folks. Who knew? Still, I had expected a bigger reaction at them finding out that they had been threatened. But other than that, they were all silent. So I decided to keep the ghost sightings to myself. For now.

I set the tea aside after I finished. "Aunt Gwen, I want you to explain to me what he meant when he called my father a coward. And what in the world is a Blood Moon Grimoire? That's not here in the house is it?"

"No, it is not." Gwen said firmly. "I've never even heard of it before."

"What happened twenty-two years ago?" I asked.

Gwen seemed to choose her next words deliberately, "Twenty-two years ago this family experienced what could best be described as a serious magickal attack, for reasons I still don't understand. Your grandparents and your father's best friend all died."

Well, holy crap. That was a bit of an unexpected bomb to drop into the conversation. I was silent for a moment. Clearly it was an uncomfortable subject, the death of her parents— my grandparents. While I was sorry to see my aunt upset, I needed answers, and I needed them pronto.

"Do you remember our grandparents?" Holly asked me.

"Nope, I guess I would have been around two when they died. Dad never talked about his family very much. It always seemed to upset my mother."

Gwen shook her head, sadly.

"Aunt Gwen," I began, "you said that magick frightened my mother. Is that why they left?"

"Your grandparent's deaths tipped the scale, you could say." Gwen answered.

"How did they die?" I asked

"It appeared that your grandfather suffered a stroke while he was driving and that he lost control of the car. He died instantly, while your Grandma Rose held on for a few days, but never regained consciousness."

"What do you mean, it appeared?" I repeated.

"Investigators decided it must have been a heart attack or a stroke, for him to loose control of the car as he did. However we have reasons to think it may have actually been a magickal attack."

"Why would you think that?" I wanted to know.

"Since the autopsy showed that he had suffered neither a stroke nor heart attack, and it was too neat and tidy of an answer. Moreover, after the accident, another driver struck one of the responding police officers who was trying to save your grandmother. He died too, and the hit and run driver was never identified." She paused for a moment. "A few weeks after the funerals, your father left with you and your mother."

Oh my god. It clicked suddenly. *A police officer had died, probably trying to save my grandmother. Could that be my ghost?* I tried to stay calm. "The officer who died at the scene, was he friends with my father?"

Gwen narrowed her eyes. "Yes, he was." She sounded surprised that I asked.

Before I could ask the officer's name, Bran walked in with Duncan Quinn and a pretty, middle aged woman. My cousins and aunt rose to their feet. Duncan went straight to me, pulled me up out of the big chair and into a hug. I sputtered in surprise and embarrassment. The last time Gwen had been around Duncan, she was very hostile. I had to wonder at Bran bringing him and the mystery woman in the house.

To my astonishment, Gwen merely nodded at Duncan and the woman and said hello.

Clearly I had passed into an alternate universe.

Duncan held me out at arm's length. "You're okay?" He must have come straight from the job site. His jeans were splattered in what looked like paint and his t-shirt seemed a little sweaty. I couldn't have cared less. As we stood there looking at each other, I felt little tingles from where his hands touched my arms.

I smiled. I couldn't help it. "I'm glad to see you, but what are you doing here?"

"Bran called me." He said, and then he addressed the group. "I'm not sure what my uncle thinks he's doing with this stunt, but believe me when I say we had no idea he would try such a thing."

"Why would he do that, use magick on her in a public place?" Holly asked.

"Power play, maybe?" Ivy threw her two cents in.

"Girls." Gwen cut off the twin's theories.

I nudged Duncan, "Are you going to introduce me?"

"Oops. Sorry." He grinned. "Autumn, this is my mother, Rebecca Drake-Quinn."

My mouth hit the floor. What happened to the whole shtick about the entire family being evil? "Uh, hello." I said.

As I studied the woman who stood there, poised and quiet in an elegant navy skirt and jacket, I could see where Duncan had gotten his blue eyes and blonde hair.

She smiled at me gently. "Hello Autumn." Her voice was as cultured and sophisticated as the rest of her. I looked over at Gwen to see how she was reacting to having half of the Drake family inside of the manor.

"Rebecca, won't you take a seat?" Gwen invited, and gestured for the rest of us to do the same.

I think my eyes almost popped out of my head at the

polite manners and calm atmosphere in the family room. Rebecca chose a chair next to mine. Bran went over on the couch by his mother. The twins plopped back on the rug. I sat in the comfy armchair again, and Duncan chose to sit on the arm of my chair. To my shock, Merlin gave up his spot, then walked over to Rebecca and started rubbing against her ankles. She reached down to pet him, and, taking that as an invitation, Merlin jumped into her lap as if they were old friends. Then he sat there and purred. Loudly.

Ivy started to chuckle at Merlin, and Gwen observed Rebecca and the cat for a moment. "Animals are foolproof barometers of people and their intentions, Mom." Ivy poked Gwen. "You taught me that yourself."

Rebecca cleared her throat and addressed everyone. "I understand that you are hesitant to have us in your home, however, we find ourselves in extraordinary circumstances."

Gwen looked at Rebecca, "Were you seen, coming here?"

Rebecca gave a slight smile, "Not at all. I used a glamour."

"Duncan?" Gwen nodded.

"I don't care if I'm seen or not." Duncan crossed his arms, and then continued. "What I want to know is why he would spell Autumn and then threaten your family? What could he hope to gain from it?"

"He said he wanted me to find the Blood Moon

Grimoire." I explained.

"The what?" he frowned down at me, visibly confused.

"No..." Rebecca whispered and went a little pale.

Duncan reached over to his mother. "Mom?" He put his hand on her shoulder as if to steady her.

Rebecca looked around Duncan and at me, intently. "You're sure? He said the Blood Moon Grimoire?"

"Yeah. He said it was a big antique book with a red leather cover. He seems to think my father stole it and then hid it. He wants me to find it and return it to him. He said that if I didn't, then something might happen to the twins." I explained.

"That son of a bitch." Duncan hissed, and I jumped. "My uncle." He clarified. "Not your father."

"What I want to know is why does he think my father was a thief? That's ridiculous! My dad wouldn't steal some moldy old book. He wouldn't have stolen anything." I said.

And that pronouncement was met with ringing silence. *Thanks for the back up, gang.* I sat there a little offended as Gwen looked thoughtful, Bran merely lounged there, and the twins were apparently having the time of their lives. Silently of course.

Rebecca looked grim. "He did steal the grimoire." She announced quietly.

"I don't believe it." I said in defense of my father. I looked to Gwen for her reaction, and she looked shocked. Her eyebrows had almost disappeared into her hairline.

"Autumn, listen to me." Duncan's mother spoke quietly but with conviction. "I know for a fact that he *did* steal the grimoire. Just as I also know that he didn't do it alone. Arthur had help."

Gwen and Bran both started to ask questions at the same time, and Rebecca silenced them with a raised hand. "I know all this... because *I* was the one who distracted Thomas while they smuggled the book out of the Drake mansion."

"Who were *they*?" I asked her.

Your father, Arthur, and my husband, David." Rebecca stated.

The room fell to silence. Judging by the way Duncan's mouth hit the floor, he knew nothing of this either. Well, we were both the offspring of grimoire thieves. Now that's sexy.

Duncan moved to stand next to his mother's chair. "Dad wasn't a Witch. Why would he have gone after a grimoire?"

Rebecca reached out and took Duncan's hand. She looked up at her son and said, "The Blood Moon Grimoire was rumored to be a powerful book of magick, and, in the wrong hands, it could be lethal." Rebecca explained. "Your father and Arthur took the book and hid it to protect you." Now she looked at all of us gathered in the room. "They protected *all* of you, and the generations to come. And the price they paid for it was high. Very high." Her eyes shimmered with tears.

"What was the price?" Ivy asked.

Suddenly I knew. The attack on my grandparents was revenge. My stomach roiled, and I felt like crying. I looked over at Duncan and his mother. I took a careful breath. "Duncan, was your father a police officer?"

"Yes." Duncan said.

I stood up, as adrenalin surged through me. My heart started to pound and my face felt hot. I looked at Gwen steadily and this time I stated what I *knew*. "David Quinn, Duncan's father... he was the police officer that died trying to save my grandmother."

"What?" Duncan seemed horrified.

"Yes." Rebecca and Gwen said together.

My heart was pounding so loud I wondered how no one else heard it. I stepped over to Duncan and his mother, and I worked hard to keep my voice steady and calm. "Do you happen to have a picture of him with you?"

"I do." Duncan reached for his wallet. He opened it and gently pulled out an old photo. He handed it over; I met his eyes, and took it carefully. I steadied myself for a couple of seconds before I looked down at it.

The photo was older snapshot, one that had been trimmed to wallet size. It was faded a bit, but the images were crystal clear. I saw a toddler aged Duncan, held in a younger Rebecca's arms. A man with dark hair cut military style short, had his arms around them both. The man was serious, but smiling, in his dress uniform, and was very familiar to me.

"Hello David, nice to see you again." I said to the picture of the man whose ghost I had spoken to not an hour before.

In my mind I heard his voice say. *You need my help, and I need yours.*

I saw black and white spots in front of my eyes. A roar filled my ears, and then I saw and heard nothing. Nothing at all.

***

Someone was stroking my hair, and it wasn't a bad way to wake up. Their voice was low and smooth, but sounded a little worried. I sighed and opened my eyes.

"There you are." Duncan leaned over into my face and smiled at me. I blinked and found that I was lying on the family room floor, with my head in his lap.

"How did I end up down here?" I wondered out loud.

"You fainted, but I caught you." Duncan explained.

Ivy leaned over my face. "It was very romantic the way you swooned."

"Back up Ivy." That was Gwen, and then she was leaning over me. "How do you feel now, honey?"

Embarrassment kicked in. "I did *not* faint." I announced to the room in general as I discovered that everyone was gathered around me, staring as if they had seen a ghost or something...

Oh wait, I was the one who had seen the ghost. Seen

and spoken to. Duncan helped me to sit up, and I took it slow, waiting to see if I would 'not-faint' again. I leaned against his shoulder as the room spun a bit, and then settled. I accepted a glass of water from Holly and sipped slowly.

"Your color is better." Holly decided. She hunkered down next to me and gently laid her hand on my shoulder. I started to feel better as soon as she touched me.

Duncan reached up and drew Holly's hand away from my shoulder. "You're giving your own energy to her. Stop. Save it for yourself. I've got this. " I jolted hard when his hand landed firmly on my shoulder where Holly's had been. A big surge of power went through me. I sat up straight, my back almost arching, as I felt a delicious shiver roll through my entire body.

I reached up, covered his hand with my own, and slanted him a look. He returned it with a slight smile. I hoped to god the family wouldn't notice that it wasn't strictly healing he was sending. His energy blended with mine, and the attraction I felt to him intensified. I squeezed his hand and he caught my signal and the energy toned down. It was hard to sit there and act all serene, when what I wanted to do was, well... jump him, basically.

Duncan lifted our joined hands and pressed a kiss to the back of mine. Our eyes met and everything and everyone else in the room didn't seem to matter.

It was Bran who broke the spell. "Hey, that's enough

you two." He said gruffly.

The moment shattered by Mr. Conservative, Duncan and I grinned at each other and then he helped me to my feet. I saw that Holly was blushing; I guess somebody picked up on that sexy energy after all.

"Autumn," Aunt Gwen asked before I even made it to the chair. "What did you mean when you said 'it was nice to see you again?'"

Well crap. How in the hell do you politely tell the guy your attracted to, who just pushed hot, vibrant, and sexy energy straight through your body, that his father's ghost has been haunting you? I stalled for a few moments as Duncan helped me to sit back in the big cushy chair.

I looked around the room at the half dozen faces watching me and decided it was time to tell the truth. It was a bit hypocritical to be all bent out of shape about my father keeping secrets from me, when I had been keeping my own. I looked up at Duncan as he sat on the arm of my chair again. "This isn't the first time I have seen David Quinn."

"How can that be?" Rebecca asked.

"I first saw him standing on the sidewalk, wearing a police officer's uniform, a few weeks ago. I thought he was directing traffic. It was the day I drove the girls home from school.

"The day that crow bounced off the windshield and stopped us when that SUV that ran the stop sign." Ivy said.

Nodding, I said, "After we got home, I saw him again, standing at the edge of the driveway. He told me to 'stay safe' and I thought he was a real person." I cringed and then apologized to Rebecca and Duncan. "Sorry. That sounded bad."

"Go on." Rebecca said.

I filled them in on the times I had *spoken* to David, and I was completely unsurprised that Bran was now taking notes on a legal pad.

Bran tapped the pen against the paper and said, "It makes sense that David Quinn would communicate with Autumn. She has a strong gift for clairvoyance. We know she can divine both the future and the past. She must also have mediumship skills. Now that Thomas has contacted her about locating his missing grimoire, all of the pieces are beginning to fall into place."

Mediumship skills? Oh jeez, from the bottom of my heart I sincerely hopped that did not mean I was going to get bombarded with other roaming ghosts. The mere thought of that made me shudder.

Rebecca stared at me. "David's been watching over you, then. Trying to protect you." All I could do was nod in return.

Duncan put his arm around my shoulder. "I wish I could have seen him."

"You will." I heard myself say. When Duncan beamed at me, I wondered what had possessed me to say that. Oh crap, *possessed.* Bad choice of words from my stupid inner monologue. I started gulping water before something else embarrassing came out of my mouth.

Duncan looked to his mother, "What I want to know is, why did my uncle choose to make his move now? If the grimoire is that valuable, why would he wait twenty-two years to try and retrieve it?"

I was wondering the same thing. "He said he wanted the grimoire by the next full moon. Is next month's full moon significant somehow?" I asked.

"There will be a total lunar eclipse in the month of October—" Gwen said to herself.

"But, the Hunter's Moon is the name usually given to the full moon in October ." Duncan pointed out. "Not a Blood Moon."

"In the old days a lunar eclipse was called a Blood Moon," Rebecca said, "due to the rusty color the moon appeared to be as it passed through the earth's shadow." Then her gaze shot to Gwen's. "The magick of the Blood Moon Grimoire must be connected to the lunar eclipses of the current tetrad!"

"What's a tetrad?" I asked.

I felt Duncan tense up next to me, and Bran was all attention. Then Bran spoke. "A tetrad, is a series of four consecutive total lunar eclipses that occur at roughly six month intervals."

"Currently we are in a tetrad cycle." Rebecca explained. "The first total lunar eclipse was in April this year, and the second is coming on the eighth of October. The third and fourth total lunar eclipses occur in April, and September next year."

"Is that unusual?" I asked her.

"Lunar eclipses come in no particular order; a tetrad itself is a frequent astronomical occurrence in the pattern of lunar eclipses..." Rebecca trailed off as she thought it over.

"It says here," Ivy said, reading from her cell phone, "that during the 21st century there will be eight sets of tetrads, and all four of the 2014-2015 tetrads will be visible in the United States. So that would make this tetrad special. This astronomy website also says that from 1600 to 1900 there were no tetrads at all."

I thought about that for a moment. "So we're thinking that Thomas wants the Blood Moon Grimoire because of the current tetrad cycle?"

"If all four of those total lunar eclipses are visible here... that would be a hell of a boost to his magick, or whatever he is plotting." Duncan said quietly as he and his mother exchanged looks. "We have to find that grimoire, if for no other reason than to keep it away from him."

"My brother has always been obsessed with power," Rebecca said looking down at her hands. She wrung them once then lifted her head. "Legend claims that the Blood Moon Grimoire can increase its' owners magickal abilities exponentially. If the owner binds themselves to the magick contained within the grimoire, under the light of a lunar eclipse they will become virtually unstoppable."

"Shit." Duncan hissed. "And if that power was boosted in succession with the three remaining lunar eclipses..."

"So to be clear, the Blood Moon Grimoire is like a magickal battery that holds a charge?" I tried to puzzle it out. "And Thomas wants to try and harness all that energy for himself?"

"That's one way to look at it." Rebecca said.

I thought back to the family's collection of grimoires and journals. None of them had been red. They'd all been faded brown, green, blue and black. I figured if Holly and Ivy weren't jumping up and off and running to go look, then they didn't think the Blood Moon Grimoire was in the house either.

"Mrs. Quinn, do you know where they hid the grimoire?" Bran asked politely.

"No I don't," Rebecca admitted and I saw a pained expression cross her face. "They never told me, and then David died a few weeks after they took the book out of the manor."

"My uncle never suspected you had a role in all this?" Duncan asked his mother.

"If I had shown any of the guilt I'd felt, he might have realized I played a part in the theft." Rebecca said to Duncan, in a shaking voice, "I sent you away to boarding school, where you would be safe. Someone had to stay here and quietly monitor Thomas. And I played my part of the devoted sister well. I didn't *want* to live here, but I knew you would come back someday,

Duncan, and I had to be here to protect you."

Oh god, they had paid a high price indeed. That price had been David's life, my grandparents' lives, and then Rebecca's freedom. I was beginning to understand why my mother had insisted they leave, why my father had bound my powers, and why he rarely spoke of his family or came back to his home town.

The legacy of my family's magick, that Gwen had made seem so attractive, suddenly didn't seem very enchanting any more.

CHAPTER 12

We had to find the Blood Moon Grimoire. Everyone agreed it was our top priority, with each of us using our own particular talents in the search. I wasn't sure exactly what that entailed, but at least we seemed to be working together. What's that old saying... the enemy of my enemy is my friend? I supposed in a way, Duncan and his mother were enemies of Thomas.

The general consensus was that Thomas Drake had probably cast a vengeance type of spell all those years ago when he found his precious Blood Moon Grimoire missing. Since he hadn't known for sure who the culprits were, the group figured that he'd thrown out his magickal revenge, and then sat back, waited, and watched to see whose worlds blew up. Suddenly I felt like I had gotten off very easily with that near miss with the SUV, and then with my encounter at the library.

Rebecca stood. "Thank you for inviting me to your home." She sounded stiff and formal.

My aunt walked over to Rebecca and took her hand.

"We were friends once." She met Rebecca's eyes and then drew her in for a hug.

"I didn't have the courage to face you." Rebecca sniffled a bit. I watched as the two women embraced, and they both cried a little. I saw Holly wipe a tear away from her own eye.

They let go of each other, and Gwen said quietly. "We owe it to Arthur, David, and my parents to find this grimoire and put an end to this."

"Agreed." Said Rebecca, and the energy in the room shifted, became lighter almost.

"We should all meet back here in a few days and see what we have learned about the grimoire." Bran said.

"In the meantime, I would like to work protection magick for Autumn and the girls." Rebecca paused for a moment and looked at Holly, Ivy and me. "With the girl's permission of course."

"Thanks?" I said, not sure if that was the right response.

The twins looked to their mother and Gwen nodded.

Ivy took her twin's hand. "I think that's a great idea. That's a source of magick that old man Drake would never expect."

"How's that?" I asked.

"Think of it like an insurance policy." Holly said. "Its magickal coverage Mr. Drake would not expect to encounter or have to work against.

"I'd like to add some more protection to the mix." Duncan volunteered. "Plus, Ivy and Autumn will be working with me at the house for the next week or so. I can keep an eye on them as well."

Rebecca smiled at her son. "Good idea. We can cast the protection spells together, tonight. Thomas will be out of the house. He has meetings at city hall."

Duncan looked to his mother. "Mom do you want me to walk you out? I can do a cloaking spell so you won't be seen."

Rebecca grinned up at her son, and it totally changed her appearance. She went from seemingly quiet and modest, to someone who looked ready to stir up a little trouble. "Duncan, I may not practice as openly as I once did, but I am still more than capable at my Craft." She patted his cheek and tossed him a wink.

Saying that, she raised her hands up in front of her face with palms facing in. Then she smoothly moved her hands back down, and out to her sides. She started walking towards the front door, and with every step she took, I watched her be less and less in the room. She blended in to the point that I had trouble seeing her. "Blessed be." I heard her say, and then I saw the door open and close as if on its own. And she was gone.

Gwen beamed over at Duncan. "That was beautifully done."

Duncan shook his head in amazed appreciation. "I haven't seen her do that since I was little."

Seriously, that was impressive. I had seen a lot of magick since moving here, but holy cats! I had a few moments to think about what I'd seen Duncan's mother do, and noted that Holly was now arranging the pots of mums in an artful way on the wooden crates all around the fireplace. Ivy had started to root through the box of decorations and lifted out a ceramic pumpkin that lit up, while Gwen pulled a long garland of autumn leaves out of the big box.

Well, it seemed to be back to business as usual. Except that Duncan was easily chatting with Bran, and the girls seemed happy. Before I could ask any questions about the shift in the mood, Gwen answered me.

"I find it best to focus on the positive. Yes, we have work to do and an enemy to defend ourselves from. We also have a sabbat to celebrate, and our lives to live." My aunt looked up from untangling the garlands and met my eyes. "We go forward with awareness, Autumn. But we do go forward."

It dawned on me then, that she wasn't taking any of this lightly. Instead she was simply, as she said, moving forward. I suppose if you looked at it that way, if we all wrung our hands and worried — that would mean that 'old man Drake' as Ivy dubbed him, would be winning. Well, screw that. "I used to do the seasonal décor at the nursery's gift shop. I could..." Before I could finish my sentence, Holly tossed me a little stuffed scarecrow out of the decoration box.

"Here," Holly said. "Add this to the mantle. Only fluff him up a bit first." I looked over and noticed that Duncan was still having his conversation with Bran, so

I adjusted the scarecrow's hat and fiddled with his shredded burlap "stuffing". While Ivy plugged in the ceramic Jack o'lantern on the mantle, I set the scarecrow next to it and arranged some gourds and mini pumpkins that Holly handed me.

The doorbell rang and I jolted. Was Rebecca back? Had old man Drake decided to come by and threaten us again? My mind raced with a dozen fantastic scenarios as Gwen went to the door with a garland of autumn leaves wrapped around her neck like a boa, and looked out the peephole. "Did someone order pizza?" She asked us with a bemused expression, and opened the door to a delivery boy who held four large boxes.

"Yeah. Let me get that." Duncan told her.

"You ordered pizza, to be delivered *here*?" I asked him.

"Do you mind?" He grinned at me. While Ivy and Holly let out a cheer.

Ah, well no actually, I didn't. I glanced over at Bran. He shrugged and then asked Duncan, "You want a beer?"

"You read my mind." Duncan said to him and went to go pay for the pizza.

Gwen stood back as Duncan paid the delivery boy. "Where do you want me to put them?" he asked Gwen. She directed him towards the dining room table, and Bran came back with a couple of bottles of beer. Ivy and Holly got paper plates and soft drinks for themselves. I went a grabbed a bottle of red wine from the kitchen. I poured a glass for my aunt and another for myself.

"I'll take a couple pieces of the mushroom pizza," I told Ivy as I walked back to the dining room. I handed Gwen her wine, and tapped my glass in a toast to hers. "To going forward."

"Blessed be." Gwen smiled at me.

***

Later that evening after the pizza had been gobbled down and the seasonal decorations had been displayed, I was back in my room lying on my black and white patterned bedspread. I thought about the yummy goodnight kiss Duncan and I had shared on the front porch. I rolled over and buried my face in the pillows with a groan as I replayed everything that had happened today... Magickal threats, ghostly visitations, past secrets revealed, witchy alliances drawn, and then an impromptu pizza party as we decorated for the sabbat.

I let out a sigh as Merlin vaulted onto my bed and then walked across my back. He nuzzled my ear and started to purr. "Hi kitty." I said.

I lay there, while Merlin did his happy feet impersonation on my back, and decided to finally put away the last of my personal things. I flipped over and Merlin simply climbed into my lap to continue his kneading. I ran a hand over his head, and stared at the last packing box that remained.

It seemed to be mocking me. *Are you in or are you out?*

I rose and the cat hopped down. I went over to the box, pried the lid up, and looked at its contents. I could identify all of the items by their shapes,— even though they were wrapped in paper or bubble wrap. The little jewelry box my parents had given me for my sixteenth birthday, my framed high school and bachelor's degree diplomas, and an ornate antique silver hand mirror and brush set. I never understood why my father had given that set to me, the silver of the mirror never seemed to tarnish, but it was useless, as the mirror was all black. However he'd told me it was valuable — so I'd humored him and kept it. Here was my scrapbook from college and all my other trinkets were still safely there.

What I was really after was the trio of framed, antique, botanical drawings at the bottom. I pulled the other items out, and then removed the wrapped framed art. I looked around at the pretty robin's egg blue of the walls of my room. Which, according to Holly, had been repainted especially for me before I had arrived. I bet those matted and framed drawings would look nice up on the wall over my bed.

As if my thoughts had conjured her up, Holly appeared in my doorway. Ivy showed up a moment later. When I asked them if they could find me some nails and a hammer, Ivy gave me a thumbs up and took off down stairs.

Which is why I found myself a half hour later,

decorating my room by committee. The twins sat and sprawled on the big iron bed and offered suggestions on the placement and positioning of the botanical drawings. Holly sat considering the trio of drawings, while Ivy sprawled, her head hanging off the bed while she napped, or possibly meditated, upside down. Like a vampire bat.

Bran stopped in the open doorway. Apparently he was living on the edge, because he had deigned to unbutton his blazer and remove his tie. "Ah, here you are," he crossed into the room, studying me as was about to hang up my large vintage botanical drawing of a rose, and held out a short stack of books. "These are for you to study. Hopefully these will bring you up to speed on protection magick."

"Thanks." I said as I stepped up on the step stool, and asked him to set the books on my dresser.

"If you have any questions, don't be afraid to ask." He suggested and then left.

Bran was certainly being nice to me tonight. Then again, he had said while we were eating dinner that he felt guilty he hadn't known Drake was in his library.

"These are so nice." Holly commented as she held the thick frames in her lap.

"They were my father's." I explained as I went to hang my next botanical illustration, this one of lavender.

From her sprawl on the big bed, Ivy announced I needed to move the nail up an inch before I hammered it in. I took a second look, she was right. I made the adjustment, and realized, as I looked over my shoulder at her to say thanks, that she still had her eyes closed. Creepy.

"Stop showing off Ivy," Holly poked at her dark haired sister.

"I'm gifted, what can I say?" Ivy replied with a drawn out sigh.

They certainly were. It was hard not to feel disadvantaged. I looked over at the new stack of books, courtesy of Bran, and hoped I would find the time between my grad school classes to give them the attention they deserved. After today, protection magick was a priority.

I went to hang the third image, this one of yarrow, then stood back and studied the results. I had always loved these old botanical drawings. They had hung in my father's office at home for as long as I could remember. It seemed right that they come with me. As it turned out, the room I now called my own, had once belonged to my father. So it was kind of a full circle that the botanical drawings hung back on these walls now.

Gwen knocked on the doorframe and I invited her into my room. When she saw the art on the walls, she went very still. "I haven't seen those in a long time."

"Really?" I folded up the step stool. "Dad always had them in his office at home."

"Do you know who the artist was?" Gwen asked me.

"Ah... No." I confessed

"Your great grandmother, Esther."

Oh. After the big talk downstairs, I looked at them a bit more carefully. I had always figured dad liked them because he was a landscaper. Knowing they had belonged to his grandmother, made them seem even more important. "I'm going to go out on a limb here." I said. "I'm betting great grandma Esther was a Witch, too?"

"Well, of course." Gwen answered me patiently. "I want to show you girls something. Give me a minute." I exchanged looks with the twins as Gwen left. A few moments later my aunt was back with a thick oversized album. She moved over to the bed, and Ivy ditched her vampire bat routine and sat up at attention. The three of us gathered around as she opened the album.

In the album were ten botanical style illustrations of various herbs, trees, and flowers. "These were drawn and then water colored by your great grandmother." Gwen explained as she reverently went through the images. They were lovely. All of the botanical drawings or paintings were slightly faded, but that only made them more attractive. I also discovered that on the bottom of each painting, there were notes.

The handwriting was neat and feminine and still legible. I leaned closer and saw that the notes were actually the astrological associations and magickal properties of each plant. Then I observed that each painting was signed and dated between the years 1925 and 1926. The watercolors were almost one hundred years old! As a student of museum sciences, my first thought was for conservation.

"Please tell me those album pages are an archival type of acid free paper." I said.

"Oh my god." Ivy rolled her eyes. "You sound *exactly* like Bran right now. Do you realize that?"

I ignored her. I double checked the position of the framed drawings on my wall. They would be out of direct sunlight where they hung and that relieved me. I walked over closer and noted that my three seemed to be in a similar condition to the remaining ten illustrations that were in the album. Also, as mine were matted, if there were any witchy notes at the bottom of the picture, it would have been covered up by the matting and oversized frame.

"So I have the rose, lavender and yarrow..." I thought about it. "What other plants did she draw?"

Gwen started at the beginning of the album and listed them off. "We have: day lily, verbena, viola, foxglove, belladonna, rowan, apple tree, elder, holly, and ivy."

I added them up. "So originally, they were a set of thirteen illustrations of magickal plants. The three that Dad had, and the ten that remained in the album."

"Thirteen is a magickal number. Do you remember why?" Gwen asked me.

"Because there are thirteen lunar cycles in a year."

Holly smiled down at the page of the drawn holly

plant. "Mom, could we have the holly and ivy illustrations framed for our room?"

"That'd be cool." Ivy said thoughtfully as she studied the album.

"We certainly could." Gwen agreed with the girls. "I'll see about having it done so the drawings are protected and preserved as much as possible."

Ivy studied the notes at the bottom of the illustration of the plant that shared her name. "Do we have the astrological associations and notes from these pages written down and recorded somewhere?"

"Yes," Gwen said. "My mother, your Grandma Rose, recorded them. I have her notes in the family's herbal grimoire."

"Is that the big green book, in the collection?" Holly asked, referring to the secret stash in Bran's closet.

Gwen nodded in confirmation and then said. "These paintings are magickal not only for the talent and love Esther imbued in her work, but also because your great grandmother noted that she used an herbal wash of each of the featured plants mixed in with her watercolors."

Well that was a clever bit of witchery, I thought, as I looked with a new appreciation at the trio of drawings that now hung above my bed.

Later that night as I tried to unwind in my room, I looked up at the old botanical illustrations that now hung over my head and thought about family. What I knew about my family — and what I didn't.

Why had my father taken three of those old

illustrations with him, when he left Missouri? He'd had them framed, effectively covering up the magickal information, yet they had been in his home office for as long as I could remember. Had he stolen these as well, just as Rebecca had confessed that he and David had stolen the grimoire from old man Drake? Aunt Gwen seemed surprised to see the illustrations again. If she had given them to him— wouldn't she have said so?

Thinking back to my childhood, I had to wonder how well I even knew my parents. My father had bound my powers, and, apparently, had sticky fingers when it came to magickal items. Not to mention that my mother had always been upset at any talk of psychic ability or the occult. While my father may have given up the Craft, there were little bits and pieces of magick that had been hidden in plain sight in our *new* life. Only I hadn't been able to see it.

Which brought my musings back to my mother in New Hampshire. Beside an occasional text about my classes at the university, we hadn't spoken in weeks. Knowing what I knew now, I started to understand why she had been so bent out of shape about me moving here to go to grad school. I wondered if she knew about my father stealing that grimoire. And if she did, would she know where he and his friend had hidden it? I looked over at the clock and figured it would be after eleven east coast time. Would she still be awake? Then I grinned. I could find out if she was awake, easy enough.

I closed my eyes and focused The Sight on my mother. I visualized our house in New Hampshire, and, as I did, a vision washed over me. *I saw her sitting on her back patio, sipping white wine with a few candles flickering on the table beside her. Then she turned, smiled, and laughed with someone.* My perspective on the vision shifted. *Now I saw a man with dark hair, run his hand possessively up my mother's arm. He tugged her forward and began to unbutton her plum colored cardigan. I saw him brush aside an ornate crucifix necklace, as he moved in to kiss my mother's throat.*

With a pop, the vision was suddenly gone, and I sat straight up in bed, and my stomach lurched. Oh god, how embarrassing! I had not expected to *see* that! Then I realized that in addition to the shock of seeing my mother make out with some guy... that I had never seen my mother drink in my entire life. White wine on the patio, late at night? Also, she absolutely hated candles and had never allowed them to be burned in the house, or even on the patio, when I was growing up.

I had always figured she was paranoid about fire, but maybe that was a hold over from my father's legacy of magick. Maybe, to her, it was a reminder of *spell candles*. Like all of the spell candles in Aunt Gwen's shop?

But besides all of that, I sure as hell did not like the idea of some strange man putting the moves on my ultra conservative mother. It simply boggled my mind. I scrambled for my phone, and waited, impatiently, for her to answer.

She answered, slightly out of breath, "Hello?"

"Hi Mom." I said, refusing to think about why it took so long for her to answer the house phone.

"Autumn! Well this is a surprise."

She didn't sound like it was a happy surprise, "Sorry to interrupt your evening. But I need to ask you something."

"No. There is nothing to interrupt. I was... sitting in the living room and reading a book." She sounded nervous, and very unlike herself.

With a flash of insight I knew that the man was standing there with her, and listening in on our conversation. That combined with her lying to me, made me a little angry. "Who's your friend?"

"What? What are you talking about?" She laughed again, and it was high pitched and strained.

"I'm talking about the dark haired man you were having a glass of wine with, out on the back patio. The one who's standing there with you, right now."

She was silent for a good four seconds. "You have always had an overactive imagination."

I managed to keep my tone light at the insult, and I even chuckled. "Mom my imagination isn't that good. And by the way, tell that guy to keep his hands to himself."

"Stop that," she said, clearly angry. She had always hated it if I talked about, or displayed any psychic ability around her. "I don't know where you come up with these things."

I really hadn't called to pick a fight with my mother, but damned if we weren't heading towards one anyway. "It wasn't my imagination that saw you drinking wine by candle light a moment ago." She said nothing, so I continued. "You're wearing a new necklace. A fancy silver crucifix. You have on that plum colored cardigan I gave you for your birthday last year. The cardigan that he just unbuttoned." I heard her breathing go ragged. "I didn't *come up with* that one. Did I Mom?"

"Stop it, Autumn." She whispered shakily into the phone.

I took a deep breath and tried again. "Listen, I'm sorry. I do *not* want to fight with you. Your private life is truthfully, none of my business. The reason I called, was to ask for your help."

"Why do you need my help?" She sounded confused.

"Tell me what happened around the time my grandparents died. I need to know what you remember."

"That's best buried and forgotten." She snapped at me.

"Well, it's time to dig it up." I shot back. So much for not arguing.

"Your father promised me... No." She said, her voice stronger. "Not ever again, do you hear me, Autumn Rose Bishop? I won't talk about that horrible time of my life. Not again and not at all."

"Mom, this is important. Do you remember anything

about Dad and David Quinn taking an antique book called the Blood Moon Grimoire? Do you know where that is?" I pressed on.

"Honestly, what nonsense are you talking about, now?"

"You can drop the act Mom. I know about the legacy of magick. I know that Dad was a Witch." I heard her start to sob, but I kept going. "I know that Dad tried to bind my powers." Tears ran down my own face as I pleaded with her. "For once in my life, tell me the truth! Explain to me what happened, and why."

"Autumn, you have to let this go. For the love of god, promise me. Leave it be."

I heard a man speaking in the background. Lover boy, no doubt. I tried to calm down, and to get through to her one more time. "Mom, this is important. I really do need your help."

"That's enough from you, young lady." Said an unfamiliar voice.

"Who is this?" I demanded, even though I knew. It was the dark haired man that I saw in my vision.

"Your own mother may be afraid of you, but I am not. I suggest that you go to church. You need to repent for your evil ways, girl."

I've said it before; sarcasm is one of my super powers. Having heard that unbelievable suggestion, from the faceless mother-grabbing bastard, I let my super power off the chain. "That's big talk from the guy who is getting my mother liquored up, so he can peel her out of her cardigan."

"In the name of Jesus, I rebuke you!"

Call me psychic, but that was the last thing I expected. "Are you freaking kidding me?" I said to him. *What kind of person actually talks like that?*

Then he started spouting off bible verses at me, and I'd had enough.

"Listen Romeo," I purred into the phone, and his tirade stopped. "If you put your bible thumping hands on my mother again, I'll come after you personal. Understand me? Now put my mother back on the phone. Right. Now."

A couple of seconds later, I heard him hand the phone to my mother. "I'm here." She said.

"Mom are you crazy? Did you hear what he said to me? What are doing with a religious fanatic?"

"I told you when you left to go back there... If you chose that path over your own mother, I would *never* let you come home again." Her tone was colder than I had ever heard in my life.

"I had no idea that you were serious." My voice shook.

"I am. Very serious. Goodbye Autumn." And then, she hung up.

I sat there in the dark for a few moments staring at my cell phone, as our conversation sank in. Then I pulled my knees up to my chin and wrapped my arms around myself for comfort. I tried to hold my emotions in. But I couldn't.

I rocked back and forth as my heart broke, and I cried quietly for a long time.

CHAPTER 13

I got through the next few days by throwing myself into my studies, both magickal and mundane. I finalized the planting plans for the house Duncan was rehabbing, broke ground on the new flower beds, and would begin the planting at the site on the coming weekend. Duncan was busy finishing up the rehab on the house, but when he suggested we go out for dinner I gave him a lame excuse.

When everyone met at the Manor to discuss how their search had gone, I had merely said that I had contacted my mother, and that she knew nothing. I felt like a slacker when I heard that Holly and Ivy had been searching through the storage area in the attic. And that Gwen was meticulously going through all of our family's journals and old spell books, looking for any mention of the Blood Moon Grimoire.

Rebecca was discreetly examining all of the books in her family's personal magickal library, also looking for any reference to the grimoire. While Duncan had checked to see if there had been any safe deposit boxes, or remaining personal papers of his father's, besides what his mother had kept — but he had found nothing. He said that he was going to go through old family photos next on the off chance that he'd find a clue there. Finally, Bran reported that he was double checking the oldest books at the University library in case the grimoire was mixed in, and hidden in plain sight.

After the little get together, I stayed busy working on assignments for my Museum Studies classes. Whenever I had any free time, I worked even harder with Aunt Gwen on protection magick and psychic self defense. I didn't sleep well. I didn't go for any runs, and basically I got up, went to class, came home, and studied. Then repeated. I claimed to be too busy to talk to Duncan, dodged the twins, and ignored Bran entirely. The only thing that kept me going was my hurt and anger.

Yeah, yeah. Anger leads to the dark side and blah, blah, blah... Been there, done that, saw the Star Wars movies. But I turned that anger into determination, and used the hurt from my mother's denial of our family's past, my abilities, and, ultimately, her rejection of me to fire myself up to learn as much as I could, in the shortest amount of time.

Aunt Gwen poured on the witchcraft lessons every evening, and I was grateful for the distraction. I worked hard at learning more about the Craft, until I was too tired to think straight. I was worried about what

Thomas Drake might do next, his threat was a hell of an incentive, and I wanted to be prepared. I learned to build up my energetic shields (which is harder than it sounds), and how to defend myself without causing harm to another. Those particular lessons left me shaking with fatigue. But when we finished, I would crawl into bed, and not sleep more than a couple of hours a night.

After several days of that routine, it started to catch up with me. Between a lack of sleep, stress, grad school, learning psychic self defense, and then my magickal studies, I felt horrible. And honestly? I looked worse. On Thursday afternoon, I sat in the window seat of the turret of Aunt Gwen's sitting room, wearing a ratty old t-shirt, a pair of royal blue sweat pants, and my typical mismatched socks. I couldn't keep this pace up for much longer, but at least it kept me from feeling so horribly alone all the time. I might be in a house full of people, but I still felt like an outsider, deep down. If my own mother didn't want me, how could I ever truly fit in anywhere?

I gave up trying to read from one of Gwen's magickal books, took off my glasses, and rubbed my eyes. Hard. Who was I kidding? My eyes wouldn't even focus any longer, and I could feel a migraine brewing. Then if things hadn't sucked badly enough, I found myself confronted by Bran.

"You look terrible." Bran said after returning a volume to the bookshelf.

"I bet the ladies love it when you talk like that."

God I was tired. In an effort to slow down the nasty headache that seemed determined to cap off my afternoon, I pulled my hair free from the French braid I had done earlier. I shook my hair out and tried to massage my scalp. Bran walked over to me, with a concerned look on his face. He was, as usual, impeccably dressed, and damned if that didn't annoy the hell out of me.

"Dude, do you *ever* wear jeans or a sweatshirt?"

"What's wrong, Autumn?" His voice was quiet, sympathetic, and totally caught me off guard.

"Nothing." I snapped back, shoving my glasses back on my face. I was so *not* in the mood for this. I stood up and started to push past him.

"Bullshit." He stood his ground and boxed me in.

"I'm getting a migraine. That's all." I lifted my hand to his shoulder, thinking to push him out of my way

"Hey," Bran didn't budge. Instead he grabbed my wrist and pulled me up short. "I'm not joking. What's going on with you?"

"Let go!" I yanked, but he held my wrist firmly, and kept me in place.

"I know something's wrong. For the past few days you have walked around here like a zombie. You aren't eating. Obviously you're not sleeping." He frowned down at me, and I fought not to let him see how close I was to crying.

"Like you care." To my shame, I felt tears spill over

anyway.

"That's where you're wrong." He picked up the book I had been reading on psychic protection. "How's this coming?"

"Super!" I snarked at him, and wiped at the tears with my free hand. "Thanks for asking!"

"Have you put any of it into practice?"

My headache was ramping up, and I was mortified that he was seeing me cry. "Well I tried to protect myself from pompous asses, but here you are." I yanked at my wrist again.

"You're only going to hurt yourself if you keep that up." He said quietly as he easily kept a hold of me, and that made me furious.

I swore at him, and he stood there seemingly unfazed. "Last chance." Bran warned me quietly as his eyes lit up with a brighter shade of green. "Either you tell me, or I'll find out for myself."

"What the hell is that supposed to mean?"

To my complete and total surprise, Bran released my wrist and then took a firm hold of both sides of my face. "See if you can keep me out."

"Don't!" My first instinct, to kick at him, simply fizzled out. He tugged my face closer to his, and as he looked me in the eyes, I felt a solid inner *click*. My heart sank, and I was unable to stop him from *seeing* whatever he wished. With a connection from his mind to mine, he read my memories and innermost thoughts.

All the studying I had done on psychic self defense

went right out the window. I couldn't even put it into practice. I was too tired and he was too strong. I stood there humiliated, while more tears rolled down my face. He could see it all. My grief over my father's death and the hurt that he'd bound my powers and hidden so much from me. He saw the anger I had towards my mother, from her turning her back on me, my new, and private, feelings for Duncan, and, most of all, my fear that I would never have a real home or a family to love me ever again.

It was a hell of a thing to have someone else in your head. I also realized, as he did a thorough rifling through my mind, that if he had been angry it undoubtedly would have been a painful experience.

But now that I knew what it felt like to be on the receiving end of walking through another person's mind, I was *never* doing it again. My headache intensified, and I felt my knees start to buckle. As soon as they did, he pulled back, and my thoughts were once again my own.

"Hang on now, it will be alright." Bran gently guided me to sit down on the floor.

"You son of a bitch." I said quietly while I waited for my head to just fall clean off my shoulders. The migraine wasn't teasing me anymore. It was full blown now, and, in defense, I covered my eyes, glasses and all, with both hands against the light.

"Holly!" Bran gripped my shoulders, and called for his sister.

"I'm here." I heard Holly walk into the room. With my eyes covered, I gave serious consideration to lying down on the rug. As a matter of fact, that seemed like a marvelous idea. Bran must have known, as he started to guide me down, so I could lie on my side. Still I kept my eyes covered against the light.

"What did you do?" Holly asked her brother in the sharpest tone I had ever heard her use.

"Holy crap!" That was Ivy and I could tell she was running into the room. I flinched when she dropped a hand on my arm. "Bran, you were supposed to find out what was wrong, not make her sick or cry!

"Migraine." I managed to say.

A second later Holly laid her hand on my shoulder, and to my surprise, I felt Bran place his hand gently on top of my head. And then — I felt all three of them pushing energy into me. Behind my closed eyes, I imagined it to be three different colors, and it felt cool and calm as it flowed over and into me. The intensity of the migraine let up after a few short moments. I took a careful breath, and I cautiously slid my hands away from my eyes.

I looked warily up at them, and then made eye contact with Bran. "The minute I can stand up, I'm going to kick your ass." I told him in a shaky voice.

"So she says while lying on the floor." Bran grinned at me.

"I won't be down here forever."

Bran brushed my long hair out of my eyes, clearly

unconcerned for his own personal safety. "Autumn, I wish you would have come to us and told us about your mother turning her back on you."

"Shut up!" I warned, but it was too late. Now the twins were asking all sorts of questions, and right then I wished I had Ivy's gift of telekinesis, because I would have thrown the loveseat straight at his head.

Holly leaned over and looked closely at my face. "You are so pale. How long has it been since you slept more than a couple of hours at a time?"

I gave up. "I don't know."

"You're going to take a nap now." Holly said with an edge to her voice.

Cautiously, I eased up on an elbow. When the room didn't spin, I attempted to sit up. Slowly. "Listen, honey, you can't order me to go to sleep."

"Nope. But I can spell you to sleep." She said standing there in her blue and gold cheerleading uniform. All pretty and pert, she sounded tough as nails.

I let out a short laugh. "What about free will and all that stuff you guys have been blathering on about for weeks?"

"I'll take the karma." Holly said as her eyes took on an eerie aqua glow.

***

I suppose she did decide to 'take the karma' because the next thing I knew I was lying in my bed covered up with a soft blanket, and it was fully dark outside. I sat up slowly and patted the bedside table for my glasses. Once I found them, I sat up against my pillows and noted that the migraine was gone. I looked at the clock and discovered it was around 7:30 at night. I pulled the light blanket up to my chin, and settled back deeper against the pillows with a sigh.

I was still tired, but I did feel better. I clicked on the little light on the stand and waited for my eyes to adjust. My head felt sore, the typical post migraine effect, but it wasn't too bad. Good grief, what a hell of a day.

My door slowly opened, and Bran poked his head in. Merlin used the opportunity to run into the room and jump up on my bed. Seeing that I was awake, Bran stepped in carrying a mug. "How do you feel?" he asked and handed it to me, while the cat curled up on my legs.

"A little better." I admitted. "What's this?" I sniffed suspiciously at the mug,

"Eye of newt." He said deadpan, and sat on the bench at the foot of the bed.

"Well aren't we a laugh riot this evening?"

"It's chamomile." He gestured towards the mug. "Drink it."

Since it was there and it smelled good, I did just that. I eyeballed him over the rim of the mug. "You," I told him, "are such a jerk."

"Still planning to kick my ass?" He asked pleasantly.

"You will never see me coming..." I threatened him.

"It isn't fun having someone do that to you against your will. Is it?" He arched an eyebrow at me.

I set the mug down on the nightstand with a snap. "Is that what that was, then? Revenge from when I scanned your memories about the hidden books a couple of weeks ago?"

"No." He said. "I hated to see you suffering for the past few days. I was worried that Drake had gotten ahold of you again. I thought maybe you were too frightened to tell any of us about it. So the girls and I decided I should try to find out what was wrong."

"So you picked a fight." I sipped at my tea again.

"I did. I'm told that I am rather good at that."

"It might be *your* super power, Sparky."

"Please." He grimaced. "Don't ever call me that again."

"I don't know..." I considered and patted Merlin's kitty head. "It seems to suit you."

"Autumn, I know only too well how much it hurts to be rejected by a parent. I am sorry that your mother turned her back on you."

"Don't." I held up a hand, struggling not to cry again. "I'm too raw to talk about it right now."

"Well," he patted my foot. "When you are ready to talk, I think you'll find that we have a lot in common."

He had a point. I never even heard Bran, or the girls, talk about his father. I knew that he and the twins had different fathers, because I'd overheard the girls talking about going to spend Thanksgiving with their dad.

Maybe I needed to find the family tree sometime and make a long thorough study of its branches.

Ivy poked her head into my room. "Good, you're awake!" She made a run for it and then dove on the bed to lie next to me. I barely saved what was left of my tea. Bran smoothly took the mug as Ivy snuggled in and laid her head on my shoulder. "Do you feel better now?"

"Anybody ever talk to you about personal space, Ivy?" I grouched at her, and tried to get her off of me.

"Sure. But sometimes even a hard-ass needs a snuggle." She laughed up at me and wrapped her arm around my waist.

"You think I'm a hard ass?" That was a surprise. "I've almost fainted a couple of times now, and I have passed out. That's a wimp — not a hard ass." I pointed out.

"You stood up to old man Drake, and fought back when he spelled you." Ivy ticked off her points on her fingers. "You talk to, and are not afraid of ghosts. You have only started to learn magick, and you're good at it!"

I looked down at her where she curled up against me. "I don't feel like a hard ass." I told her quietly.

Ivy seemed to think that over. "Maybe you need to see you, how I see you."

I couldn't think of a single thing to say to that. Now that she was right in my face, I noticed that our eyes were the exact same shade of green. If her hair wasn't such an improbable midnight shade, we'd look more like sisters instead of cousins. I looked at Bran and his green gaze was regarding the two of us steadily. I *did* have family. The proof was hugging me, and sitting watching over me. But I hadn't accepted them as my family. Relatives of my father's family, yes. But my family? Not really. Looking at two out of the four of them, I realized that I wasn't as alone as I had thought.

Holly came into the room carrying a tray. I could smell soup, and my stomach growled hungrily.

"You should try and eat something." Holly said and set the tray on my nightstand.

Ivy gave me a final squeeze, snatched a cracker from the tray, and then moved over. I took the bowl of soup and discovered it was my favorite, alphabet vegetable soup. I started on the soup, while Holly stood there wringing her hands.

"You got something to say, Blondie?" I asked my pretty cousin who stood nervously, her strawberry blonde curls backlit by the light in the hall.

"I wanted to apologize for spelling you this afternoon." Holly said, clearly miserable.

I ate more of the soup, said nothing, and let her sweat it a little.

"See?" Ivy said to me with a gentle poke in the ribs. "You are a hard ass."

"You were so tired, and unhappy." Holly tried to explain. "I can't stand to see anyone I love, that sad. I let my emotions rule my actions and—"

I cut her off. "Okay."

Holly's eyes went wide. "You aren't mad at me?"

"I guess I'll have to live with the fact that you are *not* perfect." I said with a heavy sigh. Then added, straight faced. "You've shattered my illusions."

Ivy snorted out a laugh, and even Bran grinned. Before Holly could say anything else I told her. "Holly, I can't count the number of mistakes I have made in the past few weeks, trying to learn the Craft."

"I was afraid that you would hate me." Holly confessed.

"No. Of course I don't hate you. You have personally taken better care of me than my own mother ever did." I tried to say that firmly, but my voice wobbled at the end.

In response to my statement, Holly's bottom lip quivered. With a sudden flash of insight, I had barely enough time to shove the soup bowl at Ivy before Holly launched herself at me. Merlin jumped clear, and Ivy managed not to spill the soup all over the bed, as I found myself with another cousin in my arms.

"You *do* have family, Autumn." Holly whispered in my ear.

"Damn it, Blondie, do not make me cry again." I muttered as tears spilled over. But these tears were healing tears, and I felt better for shedding them.

***

Saturday morning, the day before the autumnal

equinox, dawned cool and a little cloudy. I went quietly went downstairs, ready to leave for the first day of planting at Duncan's rehabbed house. I checked my reflection in the big mirror in the foyer. I had put my hair in a high ponytail and then braided it, so the wind wouldn't catch it, and to keep it from getting full of dirt. Over the last few nights, I had been sleeping better. I was able to actually get my contacts back in, and I was relieved that the big circles under my eyes had started to fade.

I had called Duncan Thursday night, after Holly had made me cry with a combination of vegetable soup, care, and well… love. I'd told Duncan everything that had happened with my mother, and he ended up coming over and sitting with me until very late at night. Gwen seemed cool about that. She only asked that if we were going to stay up in my room to talk, that we leave the bedroom door open.

So I talked, he listened, and we kissed and cuddled. Merlin hopped up on my bed and curled up at the foot and seemed to be our kitty chaperone. And I thought it was sweet that Duncan didn't mind the lack of privacy at all.

I smiled thinking about it, grabbed my red hoodie off the rack by the front door, and checked to see if I had everything I would need for the day. I had loaded the shovels, rakes, and hoes in the back of my pickup the night before. I was revved up, feeling steadier, and looking forward to spending the whole day with him.

I gave Ivy a few more minutes to get her butt down the stairs; we needed to be on the site by 7:00 am. I heard her stomping as she came down, and I had to smile. Ivy wore her black tennis shoes, a pair of camouflage cargo shorts, and had an olive green hoodie slung over one arm. Her black t-shirt read, 'You're just jealous because the little voices talk to me!' She topped it off with a black ball cap and her cat eye sunglasses. "Wow. You have sort of a Goth-Gardener look going this morning." I told her.

She grinned at me. "Will I need my jacket?" She asked as she eyed my knee length khaki shorts.

"Early this morning you will, but we'll be sweating before 9:00 am." I predicted.

"Do we need to pack a lunch?" She asked.

"Relax." I hefted an oversized backpack. "I tossed a sandwich in here for you."

"Psychic." Ivy teased me.

I grabbed my keys, put my cheap gardening sunglasses on, and then held open the front door. "Let's move."

An hour later, and Ivy and I were almost finished prepping the flower beds at the house. The bags of composted manure and mulch had been delivered the day before and had been stacked neatly on the driveway for us. I pulled a retractable blade utility knife out of my back pocket, and sliced open a bag of compost. I dumped it into the flower bed, and started to work the amendment in to the existing soil of the beds under the front windows of the rehabbed house.

True to her promise, Ivy hauled, dumped, and carted whatever I asked her to. We headed to the planting beds curved along the front stone path. I flipped a thirty pound bag of composted manure over my shoulder, and grinned as Ivy tried to pick up a heavy bag like it was a bag of groceries. I showed her how to carry the bag like I was, and she went staggering with the weight of the large bag over her shoulder. But the girl was game. She righted herself, stood straight, and flashed me a grin.

"No wonder you are strong." She muttered, as she hauled the bag, when I flipped it neatly from my shoulder into the flower bed. Ivy frowned in concentration and tried that maneuver for herself. Her bag sort of slid down and landed on her foot.

I hefted the dropped bag and tossed it where we wanted it. "Stick with me kid; you'll have guns by next spring." I flexed my biceps, and Ivy burst out laughing.

A wolf whistle cut through the quiet morning, and Duncan pulled his fancy blue pickup into the bottom of the driveway. "Morning, gorgeous." He called out.

"Hey." Ivy and I said in unison.

Duncan walked directly to me, and I was barely able to pull my compost-smeared, gloved hands off to the side before he swooped in for a loud smacking kiss. "You look better." He said studying my face.

I laughed a little, "I'm all dirty."

"I don't mind." He said in a low, hungry voice, and moved in for another kiss. I had almost forgotten that we were standing in the middle of the front yard, when Ivy began to make loud gagging noises.

"Jeez you guys!" Ivy complained. "Don't make me get the hose!"

We laughed. He tugged on my braided ponytail and surveyed the progress Ivy and I had already made. "What time do the plants arrive?" He asked.

"At nine." I told him, and went to grab more compost. I bent my knees, hefted the bag, then stood in one motion and flipped the bag over my shoulder. I carried it across the yard and Duncan scrambled to take it from me. "What are you doing?" I held him off with a grubby hand. "I told you, I have worked landscaping for years. It's a bag of composted manure. It's only thirty five pounds." I flipped that bag next to the previous one.

"Why don't you use wheelbarrow?" He asked.

"Because there aren't that many of them and I'm only carting them a short distance."

As we spoke, Ivy staggered by determinedly with a bag of topsoil slung over her shoulder. This time she was able to flip the bag down where she wanted it. "Ha!" she pumped a fist in the air. "It *is* easier this way."

I took out the utility knife again and made a large T shaped cut — one horizontal across the bottom of the bag and another vertically down the middle. Then, I grabbed the corners of the bag, and the compost slid out neatly. Ivy started to spread the compost out in a rhythm we had started on the first planting bed.

Duncan frowned at his phone at an incoming text then said, "The plants can be delivered now if you are ready for them."

I straightened up and tossed another empty bag on the pile. "Sure. And if you want to help, I could always use extra hands when it comes to unloading the truck and setting the plants in place."

"I'd like to have hand in planting up this yard. I do that sometimes." Duncan admitted.

I looked at him over the top of my sunglasses. "I'll get you some gloves."

We spent a pleasant, and productive, morning setting the plants in place. Duncan seemed to be enjoying himself as we worked. By noon, I was smeared with even more soil and feeling content. The beds under the front windows were planted with a trio of compact weigela shrubs that would be covered in deep red blooms come late spring.

Ivy was kneeling on the curved garden path as she arranged perennials in the crescent moon shaped bed. She was wearing her iPod and singing along to Marilyn Manson. Duncan, who had decided he didn't want to eat cold sandwiches, announced he was going to treat us to lunch, and had gone to pick it up. I moved to the little bed wedged in the corner by the outer sidewalk and the end of the driveway. Here, Duncan had built a sturdy post with wrought iron trim for the mailbox. I set a climbing dark purple clematis in place under it, where it would eventually ramble and climb over the top. I had a half dozen small pots of purple mums and a few bags of tulip bulbs to plant with it.

I snagged another bag of compost, worked it into the ground at the base of the mailbox post, and then took the shovel to mix the soil up. While I was mixing it up, I noticed a pair of designer shoes attached to a man who was standing there and watching. "Hello." I lifted up my head. It wasn't unusual for curious neighbors to come by and watch when a yard was planted.

But it wasn't a friendly neighbor doing a looky lou. It was Julian Drake. He was dressed to the teeth, and stood there, sneering at me. My heart slammed to my ribs. I stopped and leaned on the handle of my shovel. "Hello Julian."

CHAPTER 14

"Don't we look the filthy urchin?" He looked me up and down.

I moved back slightly so I could keep Ivy in my peripheral vision. She had her back to me and was singing away. I was a little alarmed that he had approached me this way. Especially after his father's magickal stunt at the library. As I studied him, I got a flash of insight that he was counting on me being intimidated by him. Well too bad. I wasn't quite the novice that I used to be.

"Landscaping is a dirty business." I said complacently as he stared at me. "I don't imagine a guy like you has ever broken a sweat doing manual labor in his life."

"Of course not." He replied and made a show of adjusting his silver cuff links on his shirt. He sounded insulted that I would even suggest such a thing.

"You should try it sometime. It's very therapeutic." I told him calmly. "I can show you how to plant mums if you like."

At my invitation he stared at me as if I was a bit slow. I was right; he *had* expected to have an upper hand with me. Wanting to prepare in case he tried anything, I planted the shovel in the grass, knelt down, and made a show of tucking the tulip bulbs into the wedge shaped bed.

I'm sure to Julian it looked like I was ignoring him. But what I actually did was ground and center myself. I had learned a few things, after all, in the past marathon week of studying. Rule number one: ground your energy before you cast or work psychic protection. I pulled up energy from the earth as I knelt there, and I felt steadier for it. Then with my hands in the soil, I visualized a bright green energetic shield surrounding me. Once I felt the shield bloom into place, I felt better, stronger, and more confident.

"If you could spare me a moment of time, Earth Witch." Julian said in an aggravated tone.

While part of me wondered at him calling me that, another part of me looked up at him, smiled cheerfully, and played dumb. "Sorry, I don't have any spare time today." I said, and very deliberately started to add the chrysanthemums to the little flower bed. The mums were healthy, strong, and were loaded with blooms waiting to open. To my surprise, I felt a little trickle of energy from the plants in my hands. *Thank you.* I thought at the flowers.

Earth Witch, he had called me. That was

interesting...

"I can see that pathetic little shield you built up around yourself." He said dismissively.

"That's nice. I've been practicing." I said, sounding like a bubblehead.

Julian huffed out a breath in annoyance, as I pulled a mum from its pot. Seeing that the roots were packed tight, I decided to make a few quick clean cuts along the root ball of the mum, so its roots could open up and spread out better. I pulled out my utility knife to do so, and to my surprise Julian jumped back like I had a rattlesnake in my hands.

"Damn it, woman! I only wanted to talk." He snarled at me.

I looked up at him incredulously. *First he was condescending, and now he was afraid?* "Relax. It's a utility knife, Julian. I'm not planning to cut you." Just to gauge his reaction, I flipped the knife up in the air end over end, caught it neatly, and watched him cringe.

He obviously was not amused. He raised a hand, and I saw red, angry-looking energy swirl and gather in his open palm. Right there, about ten feet from my cousin and in the middle of that little suburban sidewalk where kids were playing and riding their bikes, Julian acted like he was about to throw down some major magick.

"Are you nuts!" I hissed at him. "Don't toss that! There are kids around here, they could get hurt!"

His eyes wide, Julian looked at me. "Drop the knife and I'll drop this." He titled his head towards the energy ball that pulsed in his open hand.

I immediately dropped the knife on the ground next to the flower bed. When I did, he let that energy ball fade out. So as not to startle him again, I stood up slowly. I honesty wasn't worried about not having a retractable bladed knife. It wouldn't be worth a damn as a weapon anyway. The shovel on the other hand...

"You wanted to talk? So talk." I said to him, and wondered how long it would be before Duncan got back.

"Have you found the Blood Moon Grimoire?" His eyes shifted back and forth.

I checked on Ivy, she was working on the moon shaped bed, and singing away to 'Tainted Love', her back still turned to us. Knowing that Julian wouldn't see a shovel as a weapon, I casually tugged it out of the ground before I answered his question. "No. I haven't."

"You must find it. And as soon as possible." His voice was strained, and I could see that Julian was struggling with something. It was there in his eyes. He was *nervous*. Part of him hated this.

"You know Julian, you are respected at the museum. I've seen the work you do. You really don't strike me as the type to be your father's minion." I said, hoping to get through to him.

"I'm no one's minion!" His eyes narrowed and I realized that I had struck a nerve. "You have no idea of the things I can do, or even the things I have done!" And then he softly laughed.

As soon as he did, I got an intuitive flash. *His laugh.* I had heard that before, the day at the club pool when the little boy was drowning. And I knew. Call it The Sight, intuition, postcognition, or a good old fashioned gut hunch. "You used magick to try and drown that little boy."

"No!" He recoiled. "I only manipulated him with magick so he'd swim out to the deep end. He went under on his own. Your cousin rescued him, so there wasn't any harm. I had to find a way to see if you had any psychic abilities or powers. And it worked." He explained, as if that made it all better.

I could only stand there and stare at him as Julian's mood shifted again.

"You have no idea of the pressure I am under... *no* idea." He said, as his eye started to twitch.

I knew he was spoiled, privileged, and suave in a creepy way — but it was becoming very clear to me that he had an emotional problem as well.

"Duncan won't even speak to me now that he's figured it out. Damn boy scout." Julian practically snorted with derision. "He thinks too much of himself, and his morals, to work magick with the rest of the family."

"What *rest of the family*?" I asked him.

"It doesn't matter." Julian waved that off. "Listen to me," Now his voice took on a coaxing tone. "If you did find the grimoire, and you brought it to me, I'd see to it that you'd win a graduate assistanceship position at the museum. Your tuition would be completely covered."

I tried to keep up with his changing moods. "What, threats didn't get you what you wanted, so now you're going to try and bribe me?" Damn, he was pissing me off.

"I like you. I don't want to see you get hurt."

And that was way out of left field. I hoisted the shovel, blade end up, and had the pleasure of seeing Julian's eyes widen in fear, again. "You should get out of here, before I decide to test my own morals." I told him.

He frowned at me, but took a step back. "You wouldn't dare."

I raised up the shovel like a baseball bat and got ready to swing for the fences. Before I could do anything stupid, Duncan's truck whipped into the driveway.

"Autumn!" Duncan called out. He jumped out and stalked towards his cousin, with both fists clenched.

"I'm leaving. I'm leaving!" Julian said and backed away from me. "Do yourself a favor." Julian told Duncan. "Convince her to find that grimoire." Then he took off at a quick jog down the street and ducked into a fancy sports car. He gunned the engine loudly as he drove past Duncan and I, as we stood at end of the driveway.

As the car roared past, Ivy pulled her earbuds out and looked up at the two of us, blissfully unaware of what had recently transpired. "Oh good, lunch is here!"

She hopped up and was all smiles. "I'm *starving!*" She said dramatically.

"Are you okay?" Duncan asked me quietly.

"Not in front of Ivy." I said out of the corner of my mouth.

"I want to take some pictures of my flowers." Ivy said and pulled out her cell phone to take several shots of her nearly completed flower bed.

I admired the neat and tidy flower bed with its mixture of perennials and annuals. The Ornamental kale glowed purple, the autumn joy sedum added some structure and height. The yellow and white mums were bright and perky, and the pansies Ivy had started to plant, filled in the bed with a happy rainbow of colors.

I put my arm around her shoulder. Partly for comfort, and partly because I was proud of the work she had done. "You did a great job, now let's eat."

Lunch was handed out and the three of us sat on the side of the house in the shade. The planting was mostly done, and I could have the mulch spread out and the gardens watered by the end of the afternoon.

Ivy announced she wanted to finish up her planting before Holly came by to see the house. I watched her tuck her little purple garden trowel in her cargo pocket, put her earbuds in place, and crank up her iPod. She grabbed the last flat of autumn pansies as she walked around to the front yard. As soon as she went around the corner, I filled Duncan in on what had transpired.

"I think something is seriously wrong with your

cousin." I confided to Duncan.

"There's a news flash."

"No really, I'm serious. Julian was afraid."

"He's going to be the next time I see him." Duncan growled.

"No, *listen* to me." I grabbed Duncan's arm and felt that familiar zip of energy shoot up from my hand to my shoulder. "He seemed jumpy, nervous, and desperate. When I pulled out my utility knife, to free up the roots on the chrysanthemums, he literally jumped back."

"He should have been more afraid of you decking him with the business end of the shovel." Duncan brushed away my concerns, reached down, and planted a quick kiss on my mouth. "I love a woman who can threaten a man with a garden tool."

I laughed at his teasing, and then tried to relax against him. I sighed, and laid my cheek against his chest for a few moments. We stood there in the shade as he held me. Then I remembered that Ivy was right around the corner. "Let's go finish up." I suggested. I gathered up the trash from lunch, and almost walked smack into Holly.

"Hi!" Holly said. "The yard looks so pretty!" She twinkled up at Duncan and I had a moment to regret how dirty and sweaty I was. Confronted with my young, gorgeous, and fresh-as-a-daisy cousin, there was no contest as to who looked better. As if he knew my thoughts, Duncan wrapped an arm around my waist.

"Hey, Blondie." I said in greeting.

"Wow, you got so much done today! I can't wait to see Ivy and ask her which bed she planted."

"She's right there in the front, planting pansies by the flagstone garden path." I told Holly.

"I didn't see her, but I figured that was the bed she was working on. It was a mess." Holly giggled.

"What do you mean a mess?" I asked her. "Ivy's been doing a great job all day."

The three of us walked around the corner, and Ivy was no where to be seen in the small front yard. The once pristine bed she had worked on so diligently, now looked trashed and flowers lay broken and uprooted. What in the world?

"Maybe she went in the house." Duncan guessed and went to check inside. I backtracked to the back yard. "She's not back there." I said a few moments later.

"Where'd she go?' Duncan frowned at me, while Holly got out her cell phone and started texting. A second later we heard a familiar text tone alert sound, and I walked over to the flower bed where Ivy had been working, to find her cell phone lying in a clump of uprooted pansies.

I started to pick it up, and then stopped. I shouldn't disturb it. As I looked around more carefully, my heart started to beat hard in my chest. I noticed a trail of soil that was messily smeared along the flagstone garden path, and a bit farther along I saw her red iPod lying in the driveway. "Something's wrong." I said and yanked my hand away from her phone.

"Wait, let me try something." Holly said. She hunkered down next to the flower bed and held her hands right above the soil. She turned slightly back and forth and then her eyes snapped open. "Someone's taken her." Holly began to cry.

"Duncan." I said. "Call the police."

I shouldn't have wasted my breath. He was already dialing 911.

***

You know, in the movies they make an investigation from the police department seem so quick and orderly, but in reality it is not. While Duncan called the police and then Bran (God, who was going to tell Aunt Gwen?), Holly and I sat on the front porch step of the pretty little house, looked over at the mess of the once charming garden that Ivy had been so proud to plant, and held onto each other.

"I can't feel her." Holly whispered, stricken.

"You mean like a twin thing?" I asked.

"I can't feel her at all." Holly told me.

I refused to think about what that could mean. Maybe she was unconscious? "Is there something we can do magickally to help find her — before the police arrive?" I asked Duncan, as he ended his call to Bran.

"They're on the way." He said, and I knew he was referring to Gwen and Bran, not the police.

"I'm supposed to have The Sight." I got up and stalked over the edge of the flower bed and kicked at the grass. "Some Seer I turned out to be! Why didn't I *see* this?" I said disgustedly to no one in particular.

Then I felt like an ass for shooting off my mouth as Holly started to sob again. I could hear the sirens getting closer, so I went to sit with her, and I put my arm around her shoulders. Duncan walked up, and I scooted over on the front porch so he could sit with the both of us.

When the police arrived, they took over the scene. Five minutes later, when Gwen and Bran showed up, a crowd had gathered out on the sidewalk, and the police were starting their interviews. Part of me was waiting for the classic, "She's a teenager, maybe she ran off," but the police treated it like a possible abduction from the moment they showed up and saw the obvious signs of a struggle. Most importantly, the purple handled garden trowel that Ivy had been using—had been found at the end of the driveway, half under the mums I had just planted, and smeared in blood.

Once the trowel was recovered, they herded us all into Duncan's empty rehabbed house, and were keeping us close by and out of the loop at the same time. When Gwen and Holly found out what the police had me identify, they had started to cry. But I knew. Whoever had nabbed Ivy had gotten more than they bargained for. She had fought back, and fought back hard. I told Gwen that, and it seemed to steady her somewhat.

I wondered if Gwen would tell the police that we'd been threatened by Thomas Drake, but I bet that she wouldn't. I mean, unless she wanted the police officers to think we were stark raving mad. So there was no mention of witchcraft, missing grimoires, or magickal feuds in front of the police.

Eventually, they told us we could go home. The garden of the pretty little house was looking all a mess, but it was being treated as a crime scene now, so there was no point in worrying over a stray shovel or rake. Not when my cousin was missing. As we went to leave, I walked around the flower bed, away from the smeared flagstone path, and felt a sharp tug at my mid section.

I didn't question it. I quickly followed the tug, and the direction it seemed to be coming from. I started to scan the ground. *There was something here... something important. Something everyone had missed.* What was I looking for? I had no clue. But as I began to walk around the far side of the flower bed, away from where the struggle had taken place, I felt a burning in my belly. "You're warm..." I heard myself say.

Holly grabbed my hand. "I feel that." She whispered to me. "Go with it. Follow the energetic trail." She explained.

I didn't bother to ask her what she meant by energetic trail, I only followed the tug at my solar plexus and heard in my own mind; *You're getting warmer.* As if I was a child playing a game. Then the pull became stronger. *You're getting hot... so hot you should be on fire!*

The pull became almost magnetic, and I felt myself tugged sharply down. Abruptly I knelt and put my hands down in the thick grass that was about three feet out from the flower bed Ivy had been working in. I didn't run my hands back and forth, I simply reached straight down, and my fingers closed on a round metal object. I felt a thrill go through me, and I heard myself say, "Gotcha." I lifted up to the late afternoon light, a silver cuff link.

A female police officer had been watching me, and now she snapped open a little plastic bag. "I'll take that." She said quietly.

My eyes met Duncan's, and I saw that he recognized the cuff link. Julian had been wearing cufflinks when he's dropped by the house that afternoon. "I hope that helps." I told the officer. And then, finally, we were allowed to leave.

I asked Duncan to come back to the manor with us, and he nodded and followed me in his truck. I saw that a police cruiser had parked on the street outside of the manor, and by silent agreement, none of us spoke until we were safely inside the manor.

The front door had scarcely closed when blurted out what I knew. "That cufflink belongs to Julian Drake!" I said to my aunt.

"What do we do, now?" Holly asked her mother.

"I'm going to that old mausoleum of a mansion and finding your sister." Duncan told Holly.

"I'm going with you!" Bran, Holly, and I all said together.

To my surprise, Gwen was fairly calm. "That's the first place anyone would look." She sat on the bottom steps of the main staircase, and was obviously deep in thought. "We need to do this once, and do it right."

Do what? I wondered.

"Maybe you should have told the police about Thomas threatening Autumn." Duncan said quietly.

"One of the officers at the scene is a member of our Coven. She was aware." Bran supplied that information and had me gaping at him. "I guarantee the police are at the Drake house to question Thomas."

Duncan raked his hand through his hair in frustration. "Knowing my uncle, he's been in plain sight all afternoon, with a dozen witnesses to give him an alibi."

"But why?" Holly asked. "Why did he go after Ivy now?"

Bran put his arm around Holly. "Maybe because she was right there and alone?"

"I thought we had more time." Duncan said. "The full moon is still several days away. My uncle must have gotten impatient."

"But it was Julian. We know it was." I argued.

"Where would Julian take Ivy?" Bran wondered.

"I wish we still had my mother's scrying mirror." Gwen muttered.

"What's that?" I asked her.

"It's a black mirror that is used to divine the future or see into the past."

"Was it lost?" Holly asked her mother.

Gwen rubbed her forehead as she explained. "It's been missing for years..."

Oh shit. A black mirror... "How many years has it been missing?" I asked quietly.

"For over twenty years..." Gwen trailed off.

"What did it look like?" I asked her, even though I had a horrible feeling that I already knew.

"It was a sterling silver antique hand mirror — with elaborate scroll work on the back." Gwen explained.

"And the glass was all black? You couldn't see any reflection?" I said, to be sure. When Gwen nodded in confirmation, Bran and Holly looked at me as if I'd finally gone around the bend.

I ran straight up the stairs for my bedroom and everyone followed me. I whipped open my closet and yanked out that packing box where I had last seen that weird, antique silver mirror and brush set.

"Dad, you were seriously like a magickal kleptomaniac." I breathed as I tore the wrapping paper off and looked at that mirror like I was seeing it for the first time.

As soon as I flipped it over and scanned the black glass, it felt like I was falling into it. Somehow upon the blank surface, I saw a blood red moon shimmering against a midnight sky. With a squeak, I aimed the mirrored side back down towards the floor. I glanced up to see Duncan watching me intently.

"What did you see?" Duncan asked.

"A blood red moon." With shaking hands, I wrapped the mirror back in the packing paper I'd torn off. In all the years I'd owned it, I'd never seen anything in the black glass before.

"Is that what I think it is?" Holly gasped.

"I swear to you. I *never* knew what it was." I said as I held it out to Gwen. "When you described it, I realized..." I felt miserably embarrassed and tried to explain. "Dad had told me that it was valuable and to keep it. He gave it to me when I turned thirteen."

"All that matters is that we have it now." Gwen held the mirror like it was precious.

"I'll contact the coven." Bran announced.

"Yes, they should all be here for this." Gwen looked out my bedroom window, judged the sky and said. "We have less than an hour until sundown; I want to be ready to go when night falls."

"Oh, well I can hang out up here in my room, and stay out of the way." I offered.

"What are you talking about?" Gwen frowned at me. "You'll be the one to scry. It is your mirror, after all."

"Mine?" I asked horrified.

"Of course." Gwen said and then explained. "If you've had it in your possession for over ten years, then the mirror has aligned itself to you."

"Me, scry?" *What if I did it wrong?*

Duncan rubbed a hand down my arm "Autumn, your

father must have had a reason for giving you the mirror. "You can do it."

What could I say to that? "Will you explain to me how to do it?" I asked Gwen.

"As a clairvoyant, it will come naturally to you. But yes, I will walk you through the steps. And the coven's magick will boost your ability." Gwen reassured me.

"Which is why you are calling them in." I said.

"If your family and coven would accept my help, I would like to stay." Duncan said to Gwen.

"Absolutely." Gwen said. "We would appreciate the assistance."

Bran put his arm around Gwen's shoulders and said. "Let's get to work, then."

***

As night fell, the coven gathered in Gwen's family room. A fire had been laid in the fireplace and it snapped and popped. I looked around at the members of the coven, as they formed a loose circle, and saw many faces I knew and many that I did not.

I saw Cora and Violet O'Connell from the flower shop. Marie from the tattoo shop gave me a big hug before she moved to take her place in the circle, right next to Violet. I met a gorgeous young man who introduced himself as Zach. He told me he was a massage therapist. I shook hands with his partner, a tall, quiet man named Theo. The female police officer who

I'd passed the cuff link to was there. She introduced herself as Lexie. I struggled not to squirm when she gave me a steady look. A young couple came in last. The woman was very pregnant and she was out of breath, but she waddled into the room at a quick pace. They introduced themselves to me as Salvador and Maggie. To my relief, nobody was dressed in flowing black. It actually looked like everyone had come straight from work.

Along with Gwen, Bran, Holly, Duncan, and me, we had a large group. I did a quick head count and found we had thirteen Witches gathered in a loose circle. I brushed at my dirt stained gardening clothes, and tried not to feel self conscious. Gwen had told me to leave them on, as it would help me connect to the place and time when Ivy was taken.

I nudged Duncan to get his attention. "Have you ever worked magick with a group this large?"

"Back in college I was part of a grand coven." He replied.

"Do I even wanna know what that means?" I whispered to him.

He simply took my hand, and gave it a friendly squeeze. "I'll explain it to you later."

When Gwen moved to the center, everyone fell silent. She took a deep breath and then gestured towards Bran.

"Hand to hand, I cast this circle." Bran said and grasped Lexie's right hand with his left. She repeated the chant, and took Zach's hand. Around the circle it went in a clockwise direction until we were all joined.

A hum of energy rolled through me when the last hand was clasped, and it felt like the floor beneath me was vibrating. What a rush! My head fell back, and I reveled in the energetic overload from being in a circle of so many Witches. I looked around the circle at each of the people present, and realized that though they were all very different from one another, in an odd way, we were all the same.

Together, we would find Ivy. Hell, with this kind of power, we could do *anything*.

CHAPTER 15

The ritual was simple. Candles were lit in each of the cardinal directions. The elements of earth, air, fire and water were called. Fresh red rose petals, courtesy of the O'Connell's, were scattered along the edge of the circle. Incense smoke was fanned around the perimeter, and then Marie sprinkled water all around. Once that was completed, Gwen invited the God and Goddess to watch over the group's working. She addressed the group and announced our intentions for the evening's work. Then she walked up to me and held out the scrying mirror.

As to not break the energy of the circle, Holly and Duncan slid their hands out of mine. They kept contact with me and skimmed their hands up to my shoulders. I gently took the mirror from my aunt, and kept its black surface facing towards the floor.

"Ground and center yourself now." Gwen directed.

I shut my eyes and took nice even breaths. I envisioned roots sinking into the ground from the soles of my feet to add stability and strength to what I was about to attempt. Then, following Gwen's softly spoken directions, I turned the mirror over and let The Sight loose. I looked at the black surface of the mirror. *Come on do your thing. Show me the past.* I felt a pull right away, and instinctively tried to fight it.

Relax, I heard Duncan's voice push clearly into my mind. *Let your mind travel backwards in time.*

"Don't stare at the surface," Gwen suggested in a soothing voice. "Instead let your eyes naturally unfocus."

I took another deep breath, like I was going to jump off a diving board, then I heard David Quinn's ghostly voice say, *The answers you'll seek to save one in the future, lie in the past.*

The past. He had told me that hadn't he? Okay if that's where I needed to go, the past it was then. I thought about it, and visualized the hands on a clock spinning backwards. I tried again, looking through the mirror's dark surface, instead of into it. And then everything changed.

I saw Ivy kneeling alongside the flower bed. She was planting pansies and listening to her music. I saw a man walk up from behind, wave his hand in the air over Ivy, and then grab her with his hand clamped firmly over her mouth. It was Julian Drake. Ivy fought like a wildcat as he dragged her out of the flower bed, down the curved flagstone path, and towards the driveway. Her iPod fell and broke when it hit the concrete. For a moment, I focused on the red iPod, and then I was able to move past it. I saw Julian struggle to keep ahold of my cousin. And Ivy's mouth moved as she tried to shout for help, but strangely no sound came out. As she gamely tried to fight him, Julian hit Ivy in the face.

Her head snapped back, and, infuriated, she fought even harder as he hauled her down the driveway and closer to the street. Ivy reached out and groped at the big pockets of her camouflage cargo shorts. She pulled out that purple handled garden trowel and jabbed Julian in the thigh. He yanked the trowel away from Ivy, and backhanded her. Julian tossed the trowel aside, where it landed in the mums under the mailbox. Ivy was limp and unresisting now. So he picked her up, and then quickly stuffed her into the open trunk of his car. He shut it, limped into his car, and zoomed away.

Then I saw Julian drive up to a dilapidated house, and pull around the back into a big, old garage with a beat-up broken weather vane tipped drunkenly over the point of the garage roof. Julian got out, looked around nervously, and then pulled the stained, blue, double garage door closed behind him.

I felt something wet plopping on the back of my hands, and it was tears. That jolted me out of the vision. I took a ragged breath, blinked my eyes clear and relayed to the group what I had seen.

"That's enough." Gwen told me, and took the scrying mirror away.

"He used some kind of spell to muffle any noise,

when he took her." I blinked at Duncan, and then focused on my aunt. "I'm sorry. I didn't recognize the old house that he took her to." I cried silently in frustration. Holly pulled up a chair for me; I sat down heavily, and felt like an abject failure. "I'm sorry, Aunt Gwen."

"You just wait. Sit quiet, now." Gwen commanded.

I was so surprised at her sharp tone that I did exactly that. The group closed their ritual down, and opened the circle. Someone hit the lights and everyone started talking at once.

Duncan grabbed his cell phone and started searching. Well that made sense, he did rehab old houses, and maybe he was trying to figure out the location. I saw Lexie, the police officer, walk up to him. "Looking at real estate websites in the area?" She guessed. They exchanged a look, and then she excused herself and went to make a call in private.

Bran offered me a glass of water. "She will have to call in that they've had a tip to check abandoned houses. An anonymous tip." Bran explained.

I sat and sipped at my water, and tried to focus back on the details of the vision. The room felt very closed in all of the sudden. I excused myself, grabbed my jacket from the rack by the front door, and stepped outside on the front porch to get some air.

The waxing moon was bright as it peeked through a few remaining clouds, and I shivered. Not sure if it was from the chill in the air, or a reaction to the ritual, I zipped up my red hoodie. I sighed and leaned my hands on the railing, relieved to see a police officer at the base of the driveway. If only Ivy had been protected like this earlier. I could hear everyone inside talking and wished that I could have done better, given them more specific details, or seen an address or something. *Anything* more helpful. I blew out a breath as I focused again on the police officer by the street. His uniform was different from the all black that the other officers wore today.

It's David Quinn. I bolted off the porch to the end of the driveway where he stood, waiting. "David!" I called. In a beam of moonlight, his image was semi transparent. But he was there, and he smiled as I rushed forward.

"You told me to look to the past to help. I did, but I can't figure out where Julian took my cousin." I pleaded with him quietly. "Can you help me find her?"

"Where's Duncan?" He asked, looking sad.

Afraid to take my eyes off of him, I pulled my cell out of my pocket and fired off a text to Duncan that said: **Come outside to the driveway right now!** "Please don't go," I said to David. "Duncan's coming."

I heard footsteps pounding up behind me, but did not dare take my eyes off of David Quinn's ghost.

"Autumn?" Duncan asked me. "What are you doing out here?"

"Talking to your father." I explained impatiently. "He's right there, can't you see him?" I gestured to where I saw the ghost, and Duncan frowned at me.

The ghost of David said, "Duncan needs your help. *I* need your help to talk to Duncan." Then to my alarm his image started to flicker.

Suddenly I got it. "Give me your hand, share energy with me." I grabbed Duncan's hand and pulled him closer to me. As soon as we touched, all my senses went from zero to sixty. The moonlight seemed brighter, and the crickets louder. I felt a hum of energy under my skin, and the image of David Quinn, now looked crystal clear.

"Dad?" Duncan's voice was soft and full of wonder.

He started to pull free of my hand to go to his father, but I warned him. "Don't break the bond. If you do, I don't think you'll be able to see him." I squeezed his hand, and we stepped closer together towards David Quinn.

"You're so tall." David said to his son.

"I..." Duncan stammered a bit. "Dad? It's really you!"

While I truly wanted to give them time for a reunion, there wasn't any time to waste. "David, do you know where Julian has taken Ivy?" I asked him.

"Home." David said simply.

"Home?" Duncan and I both asked together.

"My home. Our home." David said, and his image started to flicker.

"Show us!" I said. "David, we will follow you. Show us where *home* is."

"Follow me." David said, and then he changed from

the image of a man to a small ball of pale blue light, which floated down the street.

Without another word, Duncan and I still holding hands, both began to run. Except for the sounds of our breathing and the soles of our shoes slapping against the pavement, it was oddly quiet. When we came to the old cemetery along side the oldest church in town, I almost hesitated.

"Are you kidding me?" I panted as the ball of light zipped right through the open gates. "Damn it." I muttered, and Duncan and I charged through the gates and ran along the little path that wove through the cemetery.

"Come on!" Duncan encouraged me. So I swallowed my deep loathing of cemeteries and kept pace we him as we hurried between the headstones.

Oh no, this wasn't creepy. Not at all. As we dashed deeper into the cemetery, I couldn't shake the feeling that this was familiar somehow... Then my breath caught in my side, as I realized that *this* is what I had been dreaming about for weeks! The dark cemetery, the moon, the overwhelming feeling of urgency, and running with someone. I had foreseen this moment!

The ball of light veered right off the little path and wove through some old trees. Duncan and I followed, slowing down to compensate for the bumpier terrain. I lost sight of the light for a few seconds and almost panicked. "Can you see him?" I asked Duncan.

"Yeah." Duncan said a little breathless, "He's not

far."

It was full dark and hard to see as we jogged through what became a little woods. Now we had to slow down, keep holding hands, and carefully work our way through the trees.

"Dad!" Duncan called out. "Wait for us!"

We scrambled down a little hill, and suddenly saw a blue shape of a man standing on the other side of a small creek. Glad for my work boots, I splashed straight through the creek as we reached where the ghost of David Quinn waited. And his ghostly image was fading.

"Wait! Don't leave!" I begged him as I tried to catch my breath.

"We're here. We are home." David's ghost said and he pointed up a little hill.

"Ivy is here?" I asked.

"You will find what was hidden." David's image became a little brighter and then he moved closer to Duncan. "I love you. I'm proud of you, son." He smiled at Duncan, and his face was lit up, as from within.

"Love you too, Dad." Duncan whispered raggedly.

"Thank you, Autumn." David smiled at us both, and reached out to touch Duncan's face. His image faded away, seeming to collapse in upon itself, and then he was gone.

I gave Duncan a moment. Hell, I gave myself a moment. Our hands now free, I bent over, placed my hands on my knees, and tried to catch my breath. "Do you know where we are?" I asked him.

Duncan shook his head and gathered himself. Hard to blame the guy. I shut up, and then, in unspoken agreement, we started to climb up the little hill where David had pointed. As quietly as possible, we made our way up and through some trash saplings, and when they gave way to bigger trees, we stumbled out into the unkempt back yard of an old house.

We both stood and stared at the dilapidated house with a large garage that faced the back. I could see light coming from the garage windows. A garage with stained blue doors, and an old broken weather vane that lay on its side at the point of the garage roof. "Wow!" I breathed. "This *is* the house I saw!" *Score one for the Seer.*

Duncan started to move forward with a growl. I grabbed on to his arm, and hung on when he tried to shake me off. "Julian's in there." He hissed. "I can feel his magick."

"Hang on. Stop and think!" I yanked him down and we hunkered by the trees. "We can't just barge in there. We need back up." I reached for my phone and then realized I had no freaking clue where we actually were. Well crap, in the movies the plucky heroine barges in and outwits the bad guy with a combination of moxie and charm. But this wasn't the movies, and I had no idea what we were walking into. Magickally or otherwise.

"Call Bran." Duncan told me. When I picked up my phone. Duncan grabbed it away from me. "No. *Call*

Bran. The way you did in the library."

"Oh. Okay." I thought about it a moment, and tried to visualize the route we had taken to get here. I touched my fingers to the grass and dug them in. "Element of earth lend me your strength." I whispered. Julian had called me an Earth Witch, so I wanted to see what would happen if I tried to link in to the earth itself. It had worked before when I created a shield.

I slowed my breathing and concentrated. The soil was rich and deep beneath my hands. I sensed a powerful connection to it. I dug my fingers in deeper, and focused my intention on Bran, on the family bond we shared, and I sent out a beam of information and mental images. *Bran! Get out here, we need backup!* I felt the call, like a laser, shoot out and find its target.

"It's done." I told Duncan.

"Good. Follow my lead." He took off running, low to the ground across the backyard.

I scrambled to keep up with him, as he silently made his way around piles of junk. When we reached the garage, he stood, flattened himself along its side, and began inching towards the nearest window. I did too. Step by step, we made our way toward Ivy. *Please be okay*, I prayed. *Please be —*

My foot jammed into something hard. Flailing, I started to fall forward. But, like on the day we met, Duncan caught me. It took all my strength to stay quiet as my toe throbbed. What had I tripped over? I glanced down. In the window light, I could see that it was an old wooden baseball bat.

"This could come in handy." I whispered picking it up. Duncan nodded, then made a hand motion for me to stay put. So I leaned against the garage as he cautiously peeked into an open window. Duncan made a 'come ahead' gesture, so I brought the bat, and walked quietly to spy in the window for myself.

Inside the garage, Ivy was tied up to a wooden chair. Her head lolled to one side, and a rag was stuffed in her mouth. I could see bruises on her face, and one of her eyes was very swollen. There was junk piled all around in the garage, and while I could see her chest rise and fall from her breathing, she still wasn't moving.

Seeing my cousin sitting there, hurt, unconscious, and helpless, I felt rage like I'd never experienced before. Then I spotted Julian Drake, pacing back and forth, from where Ivy was tied up to where he had parked his fancy car. I could see no traces of the suave museum board member. Julian's eyes were too big, he was pale, shaking, and his movements were jerky. Back and forth he went, checking his watch, stepping around old junk, and muttering to himself.

I started to shake from the force of holding in my anger. Duncan put his finger up to his lips, and I nodded, and allowed him to tug me away from the window. After we were several feet away, he whispered to me to calm down.

"She's unconscious. Hurt. " I whispered back. "Do whatever you need to do, magick or otherwise. We need to get her out of there." I whispered.

"I saw a door. It's on the opposite side. Let's see if it's open." He led the way, and I followed as quietly as I could.

The door was standing open. As we crept along the building, I toted the baseball bat along and then tripped over a big rock. I landed hard against Duncan's back and apologized quietly. *Someday. Someday I would be graceful.* I was frankly amazed at our good luck, or Julian's stupidity, at the door being open.

"I'm going inside." Duncan whispered to me. "Give me ten seconds, and then make a diversion to draw Julian out."

As Duncan eased in the old garage, my heart pounded hard. When I heard nothing right away, I counted to ten, then picked up the stupid rock that I had just stumbled over, and threw it at the side of the garage. It made an impressive thud.

I heard a crash, shout, and a scuffle, and I ran towards the open garage door. With a battle cry, I burst through the door brandishing the baseball bat, fully expecting to see Julian face down in the dirt while Duncan stood over him. As I skidded to a halt inside the garage, what I saw was quite the opposite.

Duncan lay on the ground about three feet from Ivy. He was buried to the waist in what looked like a metal shelf, trash, and old automotive parts, and Julian held a metal pipe over his head.

"Hey!" I shouted, and to get Julian's attention— I

smacked the baseball bat against the hood of his parked car with a satisfying crunch. "Get away from him!" I ordered.

He dropped the pipe in surprise, and backed away from Ivy and Duncan over to the far wall of the garage. "I didn't do anything to him!" Julian whined. "The shelf just fell on him! There was a big noise outside, and then I saw the shelf tip over, all by itself."

All by itself? It had to be Ivy. I came further into the garage, and risked a glance at Ivy. She was sitting straight up now, her eyes focused on Julian — and she was pissed.

I brandished the bat again. "Hang on Ivy." I told her. Suddenly a rake that had been hanging on the wall behind Julian came slapping down — narrowly missing him. Julian jumped and looked around.

Atta girl! Like she had told me once before, if Ivy was angry, frightened, or upset she could generate the power to make inanimate objects move. And her telekinesis had just declared open season — on Julian Drake.

I glanced at Duncan and saw that he had begun to stir. I heard a rattle, and watched as a whole peg board full of tools and odds and ends started to quiver behind Julian's head. And like a waterfall they all came pouring down on top of him. He screamed high and loud, and fell to the ground. I moved to stand between him, Ivy, and Duncan— who was trying to get up.

"You worthless piece of —" I started to say, and then

was cut off by the extremely loud roar of a motorcycle.

Suddenly, the old double garage door splintered in as a motorcycle and its rider came barreling through. I instinctively jumped towards Ivy, and wrapped myself around her to protect her from flying debris. After the initial implosion, I looked up through a cloud of dust in time to see that the helmeted driver had expertly laid the bike down.

Looking tough in jeans and a vintage leather jacket, the rider leaped up easily, and stalked over to Julian. He plucked him right up off the ground, and while I pulled the gag out of Ivy's mouth, the motorcycle rider proceeded to beat the living snot out of Julian Drake.

"Bran." Ivy croaked.

I moved to the knots at the back of the chair. "It's okay honey." I told her as I got a couple loose. "I'm sure Bran and your mother will be here soon."

As Duncan moved slowly to his feet, Ivy struggled against the knots. I saw her moisten her lips with her tongue and try again. "That's Bran!" Ivy exclaimed and managed to point towards the faceless rider while I stood there stupefied.

"I've got this." Duncan said, urgently reaching for the ropes. "Go call off Bran before he kills him."

It couldn't be.

I ran across the garage where the rider held a, now limp, Julian Drake and continued to pummel him. I yelled to get the rider's attention. "Stop! He's done! Don't kill the idiot!"

The rider's gloved fist froze in mid-swing, and his helmeted head snapped around. Then he dropped Julian unceremoniously onto the floor, turned to face me, and reached up to take off his helmet in one smooth motion.

My mouth hit the floor, when my cousin Bran shook his hair back, tucked the helmet under one arm, and glowered at me.

"Is everyone alright?" He asked in a husky voice.

"Holy shit!" I squeaked.

Bran rolled his eyes, shoved his helmet at me, and went to where Julian lay. He bent down, picked him up, and slung him over his shoulders like he weighed no more than a sack of potatoes. Bran carted him out of the garage and dumped Julian hard on the ground, while I stood there gaping.

Thinking of Ivy, I rushed back to help Duncan with the last of the ropes. Bran coolly strolled back in to check on Ivy, then took a long piece of rope from Duncan, and went back out to tie up Julian.

I could hear sirens far off in the distance as Duncan, who didn't seem to be any worse for wear, scooped up Ivy from the chair, and carried her out of the garage.

"You called the cops?" Duncan asked Bran.

"I told Lexie where I was headed." Bran said.

"You better go." Duncan told Bran from where he stood looking down at Julian.

Bran nodded to the three of us, and I handed him his helmet without a word. He put his helmet back on, walked his motorcycle (*his motorcycle!*), quickly off the property, and into the same woods Duncan and I had traveled through. We heard the bike start up, and Bran drove away.

"I'm missing my shoe." Ivy announced.

"Honey, it's only a shoe." I patted her arm.

"But they are my favorite tennis shoes!" Ivy cried, and her teeth started to chatter.

"Okay, Okay. I'll go look for it." I said. Considering what she'd been through, the least I could do was try and find it.

I heard Duncan speaking to her quietly, probably trying to keep her calm, as I headed back into the garage. I eased around Julian's car, and carefully climbed over the fallen junk and old car parts. I spotted her black tennis shoe by the chair, knelt down, and reached out to push an old, semi-crushed cardboard box out of the way. As soon as I touched the box, I felt the magick.

I yanked my hand back at first, and then I made myself touch the box again. I laid my whole palm flat against the side. As I did, a rush of power ran up my arm, across my back, and a vision slammed into me. *A full moon hung high in the night sky. But instead of a bright white, it burned a blood red color. I saw a book being torn apart into three pieces. And then I saw David Quinn packing up the box and tucking it at the back of the old metal shelf.*

I blinked, and the vision slid away. I pulled the old box into my lap, ripped it open and impatiently pushed aside layers of old wadded up newspaper. At the bottom was a wrapped, half inch thick bundle with a book-like shape. It was tied up with faded red yarn and dried herbs were crumbled across the top. When I picked it up, the bundle felt flexible, and I knew I was holding part of the Blood Moon Grimoire. *I found it!*

I held my breath as I pulled away some of the wrapping to find loose parchment pages from a very old book. The pages themselves were covered in mysterious symbols and beautiful script. One side of the papers looked ragged, as if they had indeed been torn away from their original binding. "Oh my god." I whispered.

"Autumn?" Duncan called back.

"Coming." I stood up, and smoothed the wrapping back around the pages. The police sirens were getting louder, so I had to act fast. I yanked up my hoodie, pulled my shirt free, and then tucked the pages into the front waistband of my shorts. I pulled my shirt over and tucked it in to secure the pages. Then I tugged my hoodie back down to cover the whole business. I grabbed Ivy's shoe, and then scrambled back over all the debris on the floor.

"I've found something." I said to Duncan.

"My shoe?" Ivy asked.

"Yes, but I also found a part of something *else*." I raised my eyebrows at him and patted my belly.

Duncan's eyes traveled down. "Really? You did?" He seemed astonished.

"I did."

"Show me later."

"You betcha." I promised as he leaned over and kissed me.

"Oh gross." Ivy complained from Duncan's arms. "I'm right here you guys."

"Sorry" I dropped a gentle kiss on Ivy's unbruised cheek. "How are you doing?"

"I've been better." She rolled her eyes up to Duncan. "I think I can stand up."

"Nope. I've got you." Duncan grinned down at her, "You don't weigh much, shorty. But you do pack a hell of a wallop with your magick."

"I really am sorry about hitting you with the shelf." Ivy told him contritely.

I felt a laugh bubble up at Ivy's apology, and Duncan and I grinned at each other. Together we stood in the night, and watched as the police arrived.

**

It was early the next morning before everything had settled back down. The police had arrested Julian Drake, who, once he regained consciousness, babbled on about flying rakes, attacking tools, a stolen magickal book, and a masked phantom that had beaten him. I heard the police muttering about possible drug use and a psychiatric evaluation for Julian as they took him away.

Ivy had gone to the emergency room in an ambulance, with Duncan and me riding along. Gwen didn't crack until after she arrived at the ER. When she saw Ivy, *then* she bawled. Hard to blame her. A few moments later she pulled it together, and sat stoically by her daughter's side. Ivy bounced back quickly. She gave her report to the police, as did Duncan and I. When they asked us how we had found her, Duncan said that we'd been out jogging and spotted Julian's car. Which was true, sort of. Maybe Officer Lexie smoothed that out for us, but to my relief, they let it pass. Luckily, no one seemed to notice that I had anything stashed under my hoodie. Ivy was released from the ER in a few hours with rope burns, a black eye and some facial bruises.

Once we were home, I turned the pages over to Bran. Gwen seemed impressed when I told the family how we had located Ivy, with David Quinn's help, and then how I had found part of the Blood Moon Grimoire.

She was a little teary over Ivy still, and she cried when she gave Bran and I each a hard hug. She'd even embraced Duncan, and I got misty when I saw him hug her back. Then Gwen excused herself to help Ivy clean up and to get her settled.

After a quick assessment, there looked to be around thirty illustrated and hand written pages. Bran, Duncan and I all agreed, it was best to store them at the manor. At Duncan's suggestion, Bran used his digital camera and took photos of the grimoire pages, and then downloaded them to a flash drive as a backup. I watched as Bran re-wrapped the antique pages in acid free, tissue and then set them in an archival box. Even though the girls and I had teased him, Bran's family historian/ librarian title was well earned, along with his archival supplies, and knowledge for safely preserving the pages.

At the moment, Ivy was sitting up and holding court in the family room while her mother, sister, and most of the coven hustled around preparing a big breakfast in celebration that she was back home safely, and for the Autumn Equinox sabbat.

Duncan and I sat together on the front porch of the manor, rocking back and forth in the porch swing, and watching the sun come up. I could smell bacon frying from inside the house and the voices that drifted out were cheerful and full of fun. Duncan nuzzled my now clean neck. We had both finally had a chance to shower and to change clothes. Duncan had borrowed some clothes from Bran, our masked motorcycle hero, and it was nice to finally sit still, and to relax. Together.

"I wonder..." I sighed as we swung lazily back and forth.

"Hmmm?" Duncan said.

"Why did David, your dad, call that old abandoned house, home?" I asked.

"I heard some of the police officers talking." Duncan began. "Looks like the house originally belonged to the Quinn family."

I looked up at him. "What, so your father grew up there?"

"I'll have my mother check the real estate records. But I bet the house once belonged to my grandparents." Duncan said.

"That would make sense why your dad hid part of the Blood Moon Grimoire there." I realized.

"There aren't that many derelict houses in town, but still it's interesting that Julian chose it to try and hide out in." Duncan kept the porch swing rocking back and forth.

"Interesting, as in curious. Or *interesting* as in magickal coincidence?" I asked him.

"There's no such thing as coincidence when it comes to magick."

"So, are you sure that you're okay with my family keeping the pages of the grimoire?"

"Yes, I'm sure. I don't want anything to do with them. They've caused enough trouble."

"My vision showed me that the book was torn, or divided, into three pieces." I reminded him. "So that means there are two more sections hidden out there, somewhere."

"We'll find them." Duncan gave me an encouraging squeeze, and I snuggled closer.

"We should go back to that old house," I told him. "And see if we find any clues as to where the rest of the pages are."

"We should, once the police release the scene."

Duncan mulled it over. "It was a nice property... It only needs some time and work. Dad's old family house had good bones."

"Seriously, you are a rehab addict." I teased him.

"Thank you for making it possible for me to see my father again." Duncan said quietly.

"You're welcome. If you remember... I told you, you would see him again." I slanted him a look.

"So you did." Duncan said and pressed a kiss to my mouth. "By the way," he pulled a little fabric drawstring bag out of his pocket, and handed it to me. "Happy birthday."

EPILOGUE

A week later, I raked the last of the mulch into place in one of the garden beds of the charming little house that Duncan had finished rehabbing. The young family who had put a contract on the house would be taking possession soon, so we wanted to finish up. My hair was pulled neatly back and into a braid that went down the back of my purple shirt. New amethyst earrings, my birthday gift from Duncan, sparkled at my ears, in a sort of color coordination that I actually didn't mind.

I looked over as Ivy finished planting more pansies, in the same flower bed that had been trashed the week before, when Julian had abducted her. She was moving a little slowly, and had covered her healing black eye with a pair of oversized sunglasses. She had worn them with a maxi dress, combat boots, and a huge floppy hat. All in black. Holly sat beside her twin, and looked adorable wearing jeans and a 'We're all mad here' Cheshire cat t-shirt. She stayed quietly at Ivy's side, ready to help her sister out if she needed it. Duncan was attaching metal numbers to the post of the mailbox, and Bran hauled a bag of pine bark mulch over for the girls and set it next to the flower bed.

No joke — Bran was lending a hand, and he was wearing an old pair of blue jeans and a sweatshirt with cut off sleeves. Who knew he even owned such clothes? I laughed to myself and went over to cut open the bags, and help them mulch the final bed of mixed flowers. A half hour later we were all done.

Once the gardens were finished, I stood in a loose circle with Duncan and my three cousins. Facing each other, we quietly performed a quick and discreet cleansing of the property, ensuring that the new residents would enjoy their home, without any lingering negative vibes hanging around. To anyone who drove by, it probably looked like we were simply standing and talking.

Once the cleansing was complete, the girls picked up the empty mulch bags, flower pots, and packs, and carried them to the back of my pickup truck. Holly fussed at Ivy for trying to pick up a shovel, and Ivy only laughed. Then she tossed her head, managing to keep that floppy black hat in place, and floated the shovel up, neatly snatching it out of mid air.

"Ivy!" Bran grumbled at her. "How about a little discretion?"

"Bran we just did a cleansing, smack in the middle of the yard. Right in front of Goddess and anybody." Holly reminded him.

"Well yes, but there weren't any floating garden tools!" Bran grumbled back.

The girls giggled and climbed into my pickup cab, while I snapped a few quick photos of the finished yard. It really had turned out great. I hoped the family that moved in, truly enjoyed it. I tossed Bran my truck keys, and he snagged them so he could drive the girls home. I would catch a ride home with Duncan.

We waved as they drove off, and Duncan and I stood there quietly for a few moments. Then he took out his phone and pulled me beside him. With the new little gardens behind us Duncan took a couple of selfies of the two of us.

I looked at the pictures he had taken, and had to smile. "Can you believe it's October already? That means Halloween is right around the corner!"

"Samhain." He corrected.

"Is that how you say it?" I tried again. "Sow-when?"

"You got it." He opened the truck door for me, and I climbed in.

As we drove back to the manor, I watched the gibbous moon rise in the early evening sky. The full moon and the next lunar eclipse, or blood moon, was only a few days away. Duncan saw me looking up at the moon, and covered my hand with his.

"We have time." He said quietly referring to the lost Blood Moon Grimoire that his uncle was obsessed with. The same old spell book that had caused Julian to snap and abduct Ivy in the hopes of forcing us to turn the grimoire over.

After Aunt Gwen and Bran had studied the pages, they'd discovered that the segment I had found was actually the *center* section of the grimoire. The problem was, we still had to find the rest of the book. As we rode along with the cool autumn air blowing in the windows, I realized that this quest was really only just beginning.

Not wanting to ruin a good day with talk of dark magick and evil grimoires, I changed the subject. "Aunt Gwen told me there is going to be a huge Costume Ball held in town hall on the day after Halloween."

"You don't say!" He acted surprised.

"Do you have plans to attend?" I batted my eyes at him.

"I had planned to go with you. I was thinking we should go as Morticia and Gomez Addams."

"I like that idea!" I smiled at him as we pulled in the driveway of the manor. Like magick, the gate closed behind us. I reached over for a kiss and said. "Mister, you've got yourself a date for the Ball."

The End

Coming Summer 2015
Secret of the Rose
Book Two in the Legacy of Magick Series

CPSIA information can be obtained at www.ICGtesting.com
Printed in the USA
LVOW04s1436020415

433048LV00013B/637/P